Unable to Bear
the Hypnotic Power of Him . . .

Lee closed her eyes and felt his breath warm on her mouth in the sweet agonizing moment before his lips touched hers so softly, moving to murmur her name in a way that spoke directly to her heart.

She swayed toward him, her hands against the softness of his sweater as his arms came around her, holding her gently, and he kissed her with infinite tenderness. The room was thick with twilight now, lit only by the flicker of the fire. His touch was slow, absentminded, as though he were not aware of it. But he knew, all right. He knew too much, thought Lee, about the subtle ways of arousing a woman. . . .

Recent Titles by Mary Mackie

CHILD OF SECRETS
CLOUDED LAND
PEOPLE OF THE HORSE
SANDRINGHAM ROSE
SWEETER THAN WINE*

* *available from Severn House*

SPRING FEVER

Mary Mackie

This title first published in Great Britain 1996 by
SEVERN HOUSE PUBLISHERS LTD of
9–15 High Street, Sutton, Surrey SM1 1DF.
This title first published in the USA 1996 by
SEVERN HOUSE PUBLISHERS INC. of
595 Madison Avenue, New York, NY 10022.

British Library Cataloguing in Publication Data

Mackie, Mary
 Spring fever
 1. English fiction – 20th century
 I. Title
 823.9′14 [F]

 ISBN 0-7278-5156-X

Typeset by Palimpsest Book Production Limited,
Polmont, Stirlingshire, Scotland.
Printed and bound in Great Britain by
Creative Print and Design, Ebbw Vale, Wales.

Acknowledgments

My thanks are due to the following people for all their help in the preparation of this book:

Mr. Peter Atkinson, organizer of the Tulip Parade and manager of Springfields Gardens at Spalding, Lincolnshire, England.

Mr. Geoff Dodds and Mr. Peter Bell, who make the floats.

Mr. Alan J. Biggadike, bulb grower, his wife Rosemary and daughter Alison.

And to the people of Spalding in general.

The Tulip Parade takes place every year on the Saturday nearest to the 10th of May, at Spalding, in the district of Lincolnshire which, for obvious reasons, is called South Holland.

Author's Note

Some years ago I was commissioned to write four books, including the launch title, for a new series. The editors wanted a mixture of glamour and romance, each book based on a real-life event somewhere in the world. I chose to set SPRING FEVER amid the colour, fun and drama of the annual spring Flower Festival and Tulip Parade which takes place in Spalding, Lincolnshire, the heart of bulb-growing country. Being myself a 'Lincolnshire Yellow-belly', I find the setting of spacious fenland and wide, changing skies of particular appeal. The book previously appeared only in the USA, titled A BUDDING RAPTURE, under my pen-name Mary Christopher, so I was delighted when Severn House agreed to produce this new edition and make it available for readers in the UK. My friends in Spalding will be pleased, too. As you will see from the Acknowledgements, I am indebted to many of them for the help they gave when I did my research.

I've been writing since I was eight years old, but my first full-length book did not appear in print until I was a young wife, scribbling at the kitchen table while our two small sons played round my feet. Those small boys are now grown men with families of their own, but their mother remains a word addict, happily no longer scribbling long-hand but tapping two-fingers at a keyboard. In the interim, I've produced over sixty books, under a variety of names and in several different fields.

Exploring new dimensions of fiction provides a challenge and a chance to stretch myself, literarily speaking, but I especially enjoy writing romance. After all, most of us have had (or will have) that wonderful moment when someone special walked into our lives. For the lucky ones, the feeling lasts, though it may change and grow as years pass; for others, it fades away. But that magic boy-meets-girl moment remains the same. The hope, and the dream, are universal, and eternal. Share it with me once again . . .

One

Coming fresh from the concrete canyons of New York, Lee Summerfield viewed her home with new eyes. How flat the land was, rich dark soil stretching in fields from horizon to horizon, while overhead an incredible arc of flying clouds formed restless patterns as the March wind moved by. Lee had all but forgotten how wide the skies could be in the marsh country.

Not for the first time, she wondered if she had been wise to come home without warning and to rent a cottage instead of staying with her family. But after the way she had left and the virtual non-communication during the intervening years, she could not comfortably have gone back to Far Drove Farm.

Her first sight of the cottage was a red roof half-hidden among branches, with a huge forsythia bush blazing yellow in the dull afternoon light. She pulled her white Mini off the road and onto the shoulder by the gate, pausing a moment to look at leaded windows and a porch that sheltered the front door of the cottage. In front, a small lawn was edged by a fence at the bottom of which grew purple and white crocuses.

As Lee climbed from her car, a young woman with red curls emerged from the house, smiling and waving. "Hello, Lee!"

"Gail!" Lee replied, delighted to see her old friend. Five years had added a few inches to Gail's waist, but her smile was still as warm and youthful as it had always been.

They met in the middle of the garden path, exchanging hugs. Then Gail drew back and looked Lee up and down with lifted brows.

"Goodness, don't you look glamorous! That's what New York does, I suppose."

"Flatterer!" Lee laughed.

She could afford good clothes now and she had learned how to make the best of her looks. She kept her dark hair in a style that tossed easily into place, because it was more convenient for a busy lifestyle. But beneath it all there remained traces of the uncertain teenager she had been when she left Lincolnshire so abruptly five years before.

On the porch a little boy appeared, a finger in his mouth as he stared wide-eyed beneath a mop of curls as red as Gail's.

"This is my Jamie," Gail said proudly, picking the little boy up to straddle him on her hip. "He's going to be three soon, aren't you, Jamie? Well, what are we standing out here for? Come in and let's have a cup of tea. I'll show you around—not that there's much to see. I did warn you it was fairly primitive."

"It looks fine to me," Lee said.

Stairs led straight up from a narrow hall. One door led into a sitting room, another into the kitchen, with the bathroom leading off from there. The cottage was furnished with sturdy old pieces, some of them worn and threadbare, few of them matching, but as a temporary home it would suit Lee fine.

"We've been meaning to clear everything out and put the place up for sale," Gail said, "but it's been so cold this winter we just left it. Dad's been in to light a fire every week and keep it aired, though, so it's not damp."

"It was kind of your father to let me use the place," Lee said. "I really didn't want to stay at Far Drove if I could help it, though I expect they'll think I'm odd not going home to stay."

"You never could do anything right as far as they were concerned," Gail said with a frown. "How are they?"

"All right, I think. We don't keep in close touch, not since my grandmother died. Do you know they never even let me know she was ill? There was just a letter—a month after she died. Their excuse was that I wouldn't have wanted to make the trip for a funeral, but I guess they just didn't want me there."

Gail touched her friend's arm. "People can be very cruel. Don't let them get to you, Lee."

While Lee tried to make friends with little Jamie, who was shy, Gail made a pot of tea and produced a plate of biscuits fresh from the oven.

"I made some cakes and things for you, too," she said as they sat by the fire in the main room. "They're all in airtight containers. I didn't think you'd want to start baking the minute you arrived."

"Baking?" Lee repeated, laughing. "I haven't attempted that sort of home cooking since I left the farm."

"Career girl!" Gail taunted, wrinkling her nose.

"It's called independence," Lee said with a wry smile. "I enjoy it, though I won't say there aren't moments when I envy women like you. You're nicely settled in your own home, with a husband and this little cherub." Fondly, she touched Jamie's errant curls. It must be nice to be secure and loved. A career on its own was hardly enough to fill a whole life—however successful one became, there was always the moment for going home, alone, to an empty apartment.

"Don't tell me you've never had any offers," Gail said.

A corner of Lee's mouth turned up, though her brown eyes looked rueful. "Offers, yes. But never a proposal of marriage. Maybe I should settle for the fashionable thing—sleeping around or living with someone. I've been tempted, but when it comes to the crunch I just can't. Must be my strict upbringing."

"I'm glad to hear it," Gail said with evident relief. "At least you haven't changed *that* much."

From the window of the larger bedroom, Lee gazed out, beyond the laced branches of the woods, to a big old house that was just visible in the distance. The Mill House, she thought, smiling to herself. The place had always attracted her, for it was one of the grandest in the area.

"We used to dream of living there one day, didn't we?" Gail said wistfully. "And what do I get? A bungalow on an estate. Still, I wouldn't swap Jim and Jamie for the owner of the Mill House."

"Why, who lives there?" Lee asked.

"Our local playboy, Lorens Van Der Haagen. Plus sundry blondes, brunettes, and redheads he acquires from time to time."

"Van Der Haagen?" Lee queried. "Of the Haagen Bulb Company? Isn't he a bit past the playboy stage?"

"You're thinking of his father. He's retired now and gone back to Holland, so dear Lorens has taken over. Avoid him, Lee. If even half the stories about him are right, he's a man any decent woman will avoid like the plague."

"I doubt if our paths will cross, despite the fact that we're neighbors. Don't worry, Gail. I didn't come here to get involved with any man. I'm here to work."

Gail perched on the end of the bed, her red head on one side. "Ah yes, the book. You never did say what sort of book you were planning."

"It's about the Tulip Festival," Lee said. "A history, and an account of what happens today. The big parade. Miss Tulipland. The whole thing. I've spoken to a senior editor of our British subsidiary and he thinks there's a market, certainly here and probably abroad, too. Lots of foreign visitors come to Spalding for the festival. It's a unique event in Britain."

"Even so," Gail replied, "you can't work twenty-four hours a day. I'll want to see you. There's so much news to catch up on. And—there's your family. You *will* be going to see them, won't you?"

Frowning, Lee leaned on the windowsill. "I'll have to. They're bound to find out that I'm here, and if I haven't been to the farm they'll be offended. But it's not a meeting I'm anticipating with much enthusiasm, I'm afraid."

Soon afterward, Jim Forrester arrived to collect his wife and son. A big, easygoing man, he shook Lee's hand warmly and swung young Jamie up onto his shoulders, where the child sat beaming, clutching his father's dark hair.

Lee watched the family drive away, envying them their laughter and togetherness. Without them the cottage felt more isolated and even the day darkened as more clouds swam up and spit out fat raindrops. She retreated to the warmth of the kitchen and set about preparing a meal from the well-stocked refrigerator and the cupboards that Gail had thoughtfully filled with groceries.

Inevitably, now that she was back among the familiar scenes of her youth, memories crowded around, all centered on the windswept farm called Far Drove. Her grandparents, the Freemans, had been bulb growers for many years, running the business with the aid of their son Albert and their daughter Kathleen. Eventually, Kathleen met and married a U.S. Army Air Force officer named Bill Summerfield. The elder Freemans had not entirely approved of this marriage, though they had been delighted when the union produced their first grandchild—Kathleen Anne, nicknamed Lee to differentiate her from her mother.

Lee only vaguely remembered her parents and mostly through photographs. They were killed in a train crash when she was six. Lee had been taken back to Far Drove to be cared for by her grandmother, along with her uncle Bert and his wife Jinnie, who by that time had a small daughter of their own, three years younger than Lee, named Sally.

Unfortunately, Aunt Jinnie had never let Lee forget that she was an outsider. In many subtle ways she favored her own daughter Sally over the orphaned Lee, which encouraged Sally to develop sly, spiteful ways of getting Lee into trouble. The two girls had never been close.

Away from home, Gail Weaver had been Lee's best friend and confidante, both at school and later, when Lee took a job as a junior reporter on a local paper. But she also maintained a continuing friendship with Neil Clayton, the son of a neighboring farmer.

Typical of his breed, Neil was sturdy, quiet and slow-spoken, content with his lot. He often smiled at Lee's ambitions to go to London and make a career for herself in journalism, but his teasing was affectionate, unlike the scorn poured on by Aunt Jinnie and by Sally. Lee found that she could talk to Neil and they met often, not on formal "dates" but just to go for walks along the fields or by the river. Nothing could have been more innocent.

And then came a day Lee remembered all too well: her aunt took her aside in the "front room" which smelled of furniture polish and was used only on rare special occasions.

"You've got to stop seeing Neil Clayton," Jinnie Freeman had said. "What sort of farmer's wife would you make with your wild ideas about London and a career? The Claytons, and your uncle and I, planned long ago that Neil would marry Sally. The two farms are next to each other. They'll make a decent property some day. It's what happens in farming communities. I don't care how you do it, Lee, but you've got to stop seeing him before he gets too fond of you. You don't want to ruin our Sally's whole future, do you?"

This had seemed cold-blooded, even Victorian, to Lee. At the time Sally was just sixteen and Neil twenty. Didn't they have any say in the matter? But she, too, had been afraid that Neil was growing fonder of her than she wished. She agreed to end the friendship, though her method of doing so had surprised everyone.

15

She applied for a job in London, as secretary in a publishing company. When she got it, her announcement shocked even Aunt Jinnie. But Lee's only regret had been leaving her grandmother, the one person who had been sorry to see her go.

By hard work and application she had won promotion and, because she had dual U.S.-British citizenship, her transfer to the New York office had been accomplished. She was made an associate editor and settled down to be a career woman in New York, thinking the farm left far behind along with the windy, cloud-haunted Lincolnshire marshland.

But one did not cut off one's roots so easily. This land of rich earth and wide skies had remained in her mind as a place where life was simpler. She had needed a break, needed to recharge her batteries and take stock of her life, and so she had come back. Despite all her misgivings, on that first evening she was glad to be home.

A few quiet days went by. Lee renewed her acquaintance with the small market town of Spalding, where she had gone to school, and spent some time in the library collecting background information. She also managed to arrange a meeting with the organizer of the tulip parade which was to be held in May. The book occupied most of her thoughts.

Then one evening when the sun peered out beneath a layer of cloud, sending shafts of gold to brighten the woods, she was tempted out for a walk. She had tossed a long knitted scarf about her neck, the ends dangling around the sheepskin jacket she wore with blue jeans, and beneath the dark fringe of her hair her brown eyes were wide as she sought out signs of spring. Wild snowdrops nodded in sheltered hollows and along the branches of the trees buds swelled ready to burst. Somewhere a blackbird was singing.

A crashing among some bushes made her pause and a second later a boy darted out, only to stop dead at the sight of her, as startled as she was. A slight child dressed in denim that was caked with mud all down the front, he looked to be about eight or nine. There were even specks of mud in his fair hair that glinted gold in the light of the setting sun.

"Hey, you gave me a fright," Lee said with a breathless laugh. "Where did you spring from?"

"Shush!" the boy replied, casting an anxious glance behind him. "We're playing hide and seek. He'll hear you."

"You sounded like a tornado yourself," Lee said, though in a quieter voice. "And who's 'he'?"

"My Dad. And if he sees me like this"—a gesture referred to his muddied clothes—"he'll skin me alive. If you see him, pretend you never met me."

With that, he darted away and soon disappeared among the many pathways that wandered through the woods. Smiling to herself, Lee walked on, taking no particular direction, her eyes on the ground where last year's leaves lay wet and brown, among the grass and small branches that had been brought down by winter storms.

"Rikki!" The shout came faintly through the trees. "Rikki, where the devil are you? Show yourself!"

Minding her own business, Lee moved on and suddenly found herself surrounded by head-high bushes where the path led through the narrowest of gaps between prickly branches. She stepped into the gap, arms up to protect her face, and was stopped by a sudden pressure at her throat as her

17

scarf caught on something. A gasp of annoyance escaped her as a thorn scraped painfully across her cheek.

Tugging failed to free the scarf and though she twisted and turned, trying to keep her face from the thorns, she could not see where it was snagged.

"Allow me," a male voice said from behind her and a hand reached past her. "You're all snarled up like a sheep in a thicket."

The operation proved more lengthy than was comfortable since Lee dared not move for fear of the thorns. Eventually the man put both arms round her head, swearing under his breath as he fought with the prickles that had tangled in the loose knit of her scarf. She could feel him close beside her in the confined space and occasionally his warm breath fanned her cheek.

Since his arm protected her face, she was able to snatch a glance at him and found him frowning deeply over the problem. He had to be the boy's father, she thought. A tall man, ruggedly good-looking, he had hair the same gold as his son's, though while the boy's was straight and lank the father's curled crisply across his furrowed brow and over his ears. He was somewhere in his mid-thirties, she guessed.

"I'm sorry about this," she muttered, hot with embarrassment.

"Not to worry," he replied. "It's not every day I get to rescue a maiden in distress. Hold still, will you? Bend your head toward me a bit, so I can see. Every time one bit comes loose another catches."

Obeying, she found her temple resting against his sweater, where she detected the aroma of expensive body-splash. Whoever he was, she hoped his wife had not accompanied him on that evening's excursion. It might be difficult to explain this apparently intimate embrace in the depths of a prickly thicket.

The notion of conducting an illicit affair in such a place made Lee laugh suddenly. Bubbles of amusement shook out of her and the harder she tried to prevent them the funnier the situation seemed.

"Okay, you're free," he said, his own voice warm with amusement as, keeping his arms up to guard her from the thorns, he led her out into a glade flooded with red light from the sunset.

Swallowing hard, Lee managed to pull herself together. "Thank you. I'm sorry I laughed. It just seemed so—" Her explanations trailed off as she got her first good look at him and saw him smiling, his glance taking her in from head to foot.

Even in the first meeting of their eyes, she knew he was someone special. Then with a shock she remembered his son, and the wife who must also be somewhere around.

She tore her gaze from his and ruefully looked at the pulled wool of her scarf. "That will teach me to wear something more sensible," she said. "Oh . . . you've scratched your hands."

"You've scratched your face," he replied, a finger brushing the air a hairsbreadth from her cheek. "It looks sore."

"It would have been worse if you hadn't come along," she said. "Thank you."

"Don't mention it."

Again she was bewitched by the smile in the green eyes, a smile that gave him an endearingly boyish look. She found she was having trouble breathing properly as his eyes told her the attraction was mutual. Never in her life had Lee experienced such an

19

instant reaction to and from a man, and it shook her.

"I don't suppose you've seen a boy around here, have you?" he asked, bringing her back to reality.

"Yes. He went in that direction," she replied, pointing.

A heavy sigh escaped him. "Oh, he did? Gone back to the house, I suppose, and left me chasing around like a fool."

"He asked me not to tell on him," Lee confessed. "He told me you were playing hide and seek."

His mouth tightened and abruptly the frown returned. "I'll give him hide and seek when I catch him. He was supposed to be doing homework, not bird-watching. Which reminds me . . ." Glancing around the grass, he bent and picked up a large pair of binoculars, showing them to Lee. "He abandoned these when he saw me coming. He's too damn careless with his belongings."

"Weren't you ever that age yourself?" Lee asked.

He glanced at her sharply, but after a moment his mouth curved in response. "You're right—I was just as bad. Incidentally, are you aware that these woods are private?"

"No, are they?" she said in consternation. "I'm sorry. There was no sign at the entrance to the path I used."

"Several signs were damaged over the winter," he replied. "By gales, or by vandals. It's all right. I wasn't intending to haul you off to the police station. Do you often come here?"

"No—no, this is the first time. I didn't realize . . . I've only just moved in, a couple of days ago. The cottage—over there." She gestured vaguely back the way she imagined she had come, which made the man laugh.

"You mean over there," he corrected, pointing to the side. "Perhaps you'd better let me guide you back. Are you a relative of old Mrs. Weaver?"

"No, I'm just renting the place. I'm a friend of Mrs. Weaver's granddaughter."

He turned aside to follow the path he had indicated, and she fell into step beside him. She had herself under control now, for though he was very attractive he was married, obviously, and thus out of bounds.

"Are you American?" he asked unexpectedly.

"Half-American," she replied. "I was born and raised here, but I've been in New York the past few years. Why, does it show?"

"An inflection in your voice now and then," he informed her. "I'm a hybrid, too—half-English, half-Dutch."

"Oh?" Out of the corner of her eye she surveyed his classic profile and the crisp curl of fair hair, her mind reviewing all the clues. He had said his son had gone back to the house, but the only house around here was the Mill House, to which, presumably, these woods belonged. Was she walking beside the "local playboy"?

Just as she was trying to tell herself this could not be so, he said: "I'm Lorens Van Der Haagen, by the way. Just Lorens will do. The rest is a mouthful. What's your name?"

Disconcerted, she tried to remember exactly what Gail had said about the assorted girlfriends he brought to his house and the fact that any decent woman would avoid him. But Gail hadn't said he was married. Perhaps he was divorced.

Whatever the truth, Lee knew exactly what attracted women to him; she had herself nearly fallen for that smile and the aura of strength and vitality that went with his rugged good looks. Clearing the catch from her throat, she said, "Lee. Lee Summerfield."

"I'm delighted to meet you," he said, his voice deep and intimate as he leaned slightly toward her and gave her another of those breathtaking smiles.

But this time Lee was forewarned and though she replied lightly her thoughts were dark. *Don't try that on me, you snake!*

To her relief, the cottage was now visible through the trees, its leaded windows reflecting the fading pink glow in the sky.

"I think I can manage now," she said. "You'd better go and see if your son got safely home. He seemed a nice boy. How old is he?"

"He'll be nine in June. And he may have seemed 'nice,' but I warn you he's a young devil."

Like father, like son, Lee thought. Appearances could be misleading.

"I have my work cut out controlling him," Lorens Van Der Haagen was saying. "His mother spoils him, which makes me the villain of the piece since I'm the one who has to keep him in line."

"That's a pity," Lee said. "I always think discipline should be shared between parents."

"I couldn't agree more, but it's difficult when his mother is very rarely here. Well, you're safe now. I'll go and chastise that young man for losing his binoculars. And, please, feel free to walk in the woods any time you like. Good night, Lee."

"Good night, Mr. Van Der Haagen."

"It's Lorens," he corrected.

She gave him a level look from expressionless brown eyes. "Yes, so you said. Goodbye."

Knowing he was surprised by her sudden coolness, she turned away. But she felt she had made her point. Here was one woman who did not intend to fall prey to his fatal charm.

Then just as she reached the lane a clear female voice rang through the woods behind her, calling, "Lorens? Lorens, where are you?"

"I'm here," he answered.

Looking around, Lee saw him meet a willowy, black-haired woman wearing a white pants suit. Beyond the veil of branches the woman slid her arm through his and together they made for the Mill House.

As Lee ate her evening meal, questions about the man and his lifestyle plagued her. Unfortunately the cottage did not have a phone, or she would have called Gail and asked her about him. Or perhaps she wouldn't: Gail might think that Lee's sudden burning interest in Lorens Van Der Haagen was unhealthy.

Knowing she could not delay much longer, she set out the next day for Far Drove Farm and a visit with her uncle, aunt, and cousin Sally. She drove through Spalding and out along the river road, experiencing an odd reluctance to face her family. Perhaps she should have called first, but somehow she had not relished the thought of explaining her return over the phone.

Telling herself that she wanted to take a good look at the familiar fields before going on, she pulled off the road onto a dirt track that led up onto the floodbank penning the river. As she left the car, a brisk cold wind swept across the land, making her huddle into her sheepskin jacket as she climbed the flood-bank.

The sky, tossed with clouds, dominated the landscape, and toward the coast a rainstorm showed like a bruise. Braced against the wind, Lee let her eye travel across miles of plowed fields quartered by the straight lines of dykes. Here and there a huddle of trees and houses, with church spires rising, showed the location of a village.

Smiling to herself, Lee remembered the myth that, despite all the drainage, local people still had webbed feet. She looked down at her own neat feet in high-heeled boots. And in the grass, close by a growth of bushes, she saw a bedraggled snowdrop which had been crushed by some careless foot. She bent to touch the bruised flower, feeling an affinity with it. Once she, too, had been trusting and innocent, trying to grow in less than ideal conditions. And she, too, had been hurt by forces she did not entirely understand.

The blustering wind hid the sound of an approaching car and her first warning of the arrival of other people was the slam of a door and a female voice crying, "Gosh, it's windy!"

A young woman came into sight, running up the bank, her pale hair flying as she threw out her arms and spun around, laughing. Lee froze, crouched over the snowdrop, for despite the passage of five years she recognized that slender figure with its ash blond hair. Grown into a beauty from a gawky six-teen-year-old, the young woman was Lee's cousin Sally Freeman.

"It's wonderful up here!" she cried. "Feel the wind in your face."

A man came into sight, striding with lithe ease up the bank, and Lee's heart almost stopped as the tall, fair-haired Lorens Van Der Haagen smiled at her cousin and said something that came indistinctly on the wind.

Feeling guilty at being an unobserved witness, but unable to move, Lee watched as Sally tossed her hair flirtatiously and laughed up at her companion. Slim hands fastened in the lapel of his coat and she seemed to be speaking cajolingly, lifting her face to his. Her arms slid round his neck as he bent to kiss her, pulling her close to him, and the horrified Lee held her breath in disbelief. Only yesterday Lorens Van Der Haagen had been entertaining a woman with long black hair. Now he was with Sally Freeman.

Then Sally whirled away, flustered and laughing, and with an exaggerated shiver ran back down the bank. Lorens Van Der Haagen followed more slowly. This time Lee heard the car's engine roar into life and as she forced her stiff legs erect a sleek dark blue Jaguar cruised away along the road that led to town.

Two

The road ran through fields where some crops were beginning to show in thin greed rows and young daffodils lifted long leaves. A couple of rabbits chased across dark furrows and a male pheasant, colors scintillating along his sides, pecked after food. Ahead, a double row of poplars guarded the site of Far Drove Farm. Its sprawling barns and greenhouses spread beside the main yard where the rambling house stood back from the road.

A gateless entry led across a ditch into the concrete expanse where a tractor and trailer stood laden with boxes of bunched daffodils. Lee pulled into a corner and saw that the lace curtains at the kitchen window moved briefly aside as someone peered out.

Before she reached the house, her uncle came out garbed in worn tweeds, his thin hair plastered across a growing bald spot. He was a ruddy-faced man, placid and uncomplaining, but not given much to smiling. With a polite nod at Lee, he made for the tractor, then suddenly stopped and spun around as he registered her identity.

In the same moment, she became aware of her aunt's thin form in the doorway. She looked from one to the other of them, hoping her smile didn't look as uncertain as it felt.

"Hello," she said.

"Good Lord!" her uncle exclaimed, scratching his head. "It *is* you. I hardly knew you, girl. Why on earth didn't you let us know you were coming?"

"I thought it would be a surprise," Lee said, glancing at her aunt. "Hello, Aunt Jinnie. How are you?"

"Look—" her uncle said, shaking his head. "I'm in a hurry to get these daffs delivered. You'll have to excuse me. But I'll see you later. You're looking well, Lee."

"So are you." Smiling fondly, she watched as he climbed into the cab of the tractor and set the motor rumbling.

Jinnie Freeman wore the disapproving frown that had driven lines into her face. Thin features gave her the appearance of a bad-tempered weasel and though she was not fifty she looked much older, both in face and dress. She wore her graying hair pulled back with an elastic band, and a pink apron protected her plain skirt and blouse.

"You might have warned us," she said, a work-worn hand touching her hair before smoothing the apron self-consciously. "Well, you'd better come in."

"Thank you. I did consider phoning, but . . ." Lee spread her hands and gave a little laugh. "Anyway, here I am."

"It's just like you to be erratic," her aunt said.

Inside the familiar kitchen, little had changed. A coal stove sent out warmth that encompassed a big scrubbed table and old Welsh dresser where willow pattern china was displayed. The room was almost forbiddingly neat, with herbs and dried fruit hanging from ceiling beams. One saddening change, which struck Lee with a force she had not expected, was the emptiness of the rocking chair in the corner, where her grandmother used to sit.

27

A basket behind the rocker creaked as the old Labrador Jed climbed out and came padding to investigate Lee's boots, his muzzle grayer than she remembered. As she bent to rub his ear, foolish tears stung behind her eyes.

An awkward silence developed as the dog limped back to his basket. Lee felt like a stranger, though that was hardly surprising. Glancing again at the empty rocking chair, she felt the same reaction of grief and fury that had filled her when she received the news of her grandmother's death two years before.

"I'll make some tea," her aunt said. "You'd better sit down." Giving Lee a look that mentally priced her clothes, Jinnie moved to fill the kettle. "Well! I can't believe you've turned up after all this time without a word of warning. The spare bed's not aired."

"Oh, I won't be staying," Lee said. "Not here, at least. I wouldn't put you to that trouble. I plan to be in the area for a few months, doing some research."

"Research?" her aunt said as if she had never heard the word before. "What for?"

"I'm going to write a book, a history of the Tulip Festival."

"I can't imagine anybody being interested in that," Jinnie Freeman said.

"Well, we won't know until I try. It's not just a local event, Aunt Jinnie. People come from all over the world to see it."

Her aunt spooned tea into a large brown pot. "I suppose you know best. You've worked for publishers long enough. What about that fancy job of yours? Have they promoted you?"

"There are some changes being made. I've been offered a better position, but it won't start until the fall—I mean the autumn."

"A better position, eh?" her aunt said, her mouth becoming even more pinched. "With more money, I suppose. You look as if you're doing very well for yourself already. Especially if you can afford to take a few months off."

"Yes," Lee said, containing a sigh. There was no point in explaining; her aunt wouldn't understand. "Anyway, when I wrote and told Gail what I was planning—Do you remember Gail Weaver? She's Gail Forrester now—she said that her father had a cottage available for rent. It seemed a better idea than inconveniencing you and uncle Bert. I shall be out a lot, and when I'm at home I'll be working on my notes."

"I see. Well, since it's arranged there's not much I can say, but you'd have been welcome here."

About as welcome as the mosquitoes, Lee thought. "That's kind of you, Aunt Jinnie, but I know how busy you are."

Jinnie poured boiling water into the big pot, then brought cups and plates to the table along with a large seed cake with a chunk already cut from it. "Yes, I never have a minute to myself, and Sally's no more help than you used to be. You young people seem afraid of hard work. But when the mood takes her she's a good little cook, and she loves dressmaking. She's more practical than you ever were."

Lee smiled bitterly to herself. She was hardly through the door and here was Aunt Jinnie needling as always. Unable to stop herself, she said, "I thought I saw Sally down the road—with a man in a blue Jaguar."

"Yes, you probably did," her aunt agreed. "Mr. Van Der Haagen gave her a lift into town."

He was doing a little more than giving her a lift, Lee thought, and perhaps her face expressed something of her disquiet, for her aunt said sharply:

"She always has a guitar lesson on her half-day off from the boutique. Usually her Dad takes her, or Neil Clayton, but neither of them were available so Mr. Van Der Haagen kindly offered. He happened to be here on business. Don't you try making something out of nothing, young lady. You know nothing about it."

"All I said was—"

"He's a charming man, a gentleman," her aunt went on. "I know what they say about him, but I say speak as you find. Do you think I'd let our Sally go with him if I thought he couldn't be trusted?"

"No, I'm sure you wouldn't," Lee said. "I didn't mean—"

"Anyway," her aunt broke in again, "our Sally isn't stupid, you know."

That was the opinion of a doting mother. More objective people could see that Sally had always been flighty, never bothering to consider the consequences of her actions. Of course, she had been a willing participant in that riverside embrace, but knowing how naïve Sally was it looked to Lee like a case of the innocent country girl swept off her feet by a smooth charmer with too much money and no scruples.

"Besides," her aunt added, "Sally's going out with Neil Clayton. We expect them to name the day very soon, but they're being a bit discreet because his father died a couple of months ago."

"I didn't know," Lee said quietly, saddened by the news of Mr. Clayton's death. "What happened?"

"Oh, he was in and out of hospital for a year or more, but it was pneumonia that took him. His wife's broken up. I know—she talks to me. Their family and ours have always been good friends. We'll all be glad to see Sally and Neil settle down together."

Nothing had really changed, it seemed; everyone confidently expected Sally to marry Neil, whether the pair wished it or not. Neil would probably do what was expected, but Sally was another matter. Spoiled and willful, she went her own way. And only half an hour ago she had been down by the river openly inviting the attentions of an entirely unsuitable man.

Before Lee left the farm, she promised to return for tea the following Sunday, when her uncle and Sally would be present. She drove away without a backward glance, glad to have the first encounter over.

Half a mile along the road, a tractor was pulled onto the shoulder, its driver leaning on the wheel. His eyes met Lee's and she knew he had been waiting for her. She drew up behind the tractor and left her car as the young man climbed down from his cab.

Neil Clayton stood with hands deep in the pockets of worn corduroy. Pulled threads stuck out from his thick sweater and he wore a flat cap pulled low over his brow. Beneath the cap, his eyes danced with a slow twinkle.

"I thought it was you, when you went by earlier," he said. "I was in that field over there, checking the crop."

"How on earth did you recognize me?" Lee asked in genuine surprise.

Neil shrugged broad shoulders. "Instinct, maybe. How are you, Lee? You certainly look fit enough. Are you here for a holiday?"

"No, not really. A working break, you might say."

"They didn't tell me you were coming."

"They didn't know," she said, making a face.

Neil's answering grin told her that he understood perfectly. "How was it?"

"Sticky," she admitted. "Fortunately I'm not staying there. I've rented a cottage. And how are things with you? I was sorry to hear about your father."

"Thanks. Yes, it was a shock. We all thought he was getting better. But these things happen. Mother's been the worst affected, but now she's bearing up pretty well."

"Perhaps you should give her something to look forward to," Lee said. "A wedding, perhaps."

Giving her a rueful grin, he considered his muddy boots for a moment. "Has your aunt been on about Sally and me again? I wouldn't have any objections, but Sally's got to agree to it, too. At the moment she's enjoying herself. Did you know she's reached the finals of the Miss Tulipland competition? She's certain she's going to win."

"And will she?" Lee asked.

"She might—if Lorens Van Der Haagen has anything to do with it. He's been paying her a lot of attention lately, and he just happens to be on the panel of judges."

Oh, Lord! Lee sighed to herself. Was that why Sally was flirting with the man, to influence his choice in the beauty competition? Didn't Sally realize she was playing with fire?

"You saw how things are with them," Neil was saying. "I saw you come out from behind those bushes after they'd gone."

Horrified, Lee glanced at the floodbank, which formed the highest point in all that flat landscape. Anyone up there would be clearly visible to someone standing in the field where Neil had been.

"You saw them, too?" she asked. "And how did you feel?"

Neil shrugged. "Annoyed, I suppose. But what can I do about it? Challenge him to a fist fight? Shotguns at dawn? No, Lee, if I interfere Sally'll only be angry with me. I'm prepared to wait. Some day she'll get tired of messing around."

"But he's a well-know womanizer!" Lee cried. "She'll only get hurt. Don't you care?"

"Of course I care. But she's twenty-one. She'd never forgive me if I started throwing my weight around."

Lee could hardly believe his complacency, although it was typical of him. Neil always hung back, so afraid of doing the wrong thing that he ended up doing nothing.

Glancing up at the cloud-tossed sky, she huddled deeper into her jacket. "It's cold. I'd better be going."

"It's nice to see you, anyway. Drop in at Highdyke some time. Mum'll be glad of someone different to talk to. And . . . don't let your aunt get you down. You know what's wrong with her, don't you? It's guilt, basically."

Surprised by this assertion, Lee peered at him. "You think so?"

"It has to be," Neil said. "Half that farm should have been yours, since your mother was a Freeman. But you got nothing."

"I never wanted the farm," Lee said quietly. "It never even occurred to me."

"No," he said, watching her thoughtfully. "You're not the grasping sort, are you? Which probably makes your aunt feel even worse. Did she give you the things your Gran left for you?"

Sighing, Lee glanced back along the road. "I didn't think to ask. When she wrote and told me Gran had died she did say something about a keepsake, but—"

"A keepsake!" he exclaimed. "Only the Georgian silver tea set and all her jewelry!"

Lee felt sick. Here was more trouble, for the Georgian silver tea set was probably the most valuable thing at the farm.

"What did she leave to Sally?" she asked.

"Her money—a few hundred pounds, which Sally has spent. Your Gran was no fool. She knew you'd treasure her things. You must lay claim to them, Lee."

"Yes, I will," she said. "I'll see about it when I come back on Sunday. And thanks, Neil. If you hadn't reminded me I might have forgotten all about it."

On the way back to the cottage, Lee called at the neat estate on the outskirts of Spalding where Gail lived in a two-bedroom bungalow. Behind the gate, young Jamie trundled up and down the short drive on a tricycle, and Gail herself was in the kitchen, folding a huge pile of wash she had just brought in from the garden. The place smelt cheerfully of soap powder and baking pies, and Lee set about helping her friend with the folding while they talked over her visit to Far Drove and her meeting with Neil.

"And there's another thing," Lee said, smoothing down a tiny pair of dungarees before laying them on the pile for ironing. "Quite by accident, I saw my cousin Sally with Lorens Van Der Haagen. It looks as if he's got her marked down as the next conquest on his list."

At this news Gail's mouth dropped open. "Where did you see them? What were they doing?"

"They were by the river. Kissing each other. Gail . . . what you told me about him—is it true?"

"Of course it's true. My mother's neighbor goes to the Mill House two or three times a week to help the housekeeper. She knows what goes on."

"Is he divorced?"

"That I don't know, but his wife doesn't live with him. She's been known to visit, briefly, either to fetch Rikki or bring him home. That poor little chap gets shuttled back and forth between his father and his mother."

"Has his mother got long black hair?" Lee asked.

"No, she's a blonde. Why?"

"Because only last night I saw Mr. Van Der Haagen with a ravishing brunette in the woods. If she wasn't his wife—"

"She'd be the latest girlfriend," Gail said disgustedly. "Probably just a one-night stand, or a few days' diversion before he goes on to the next. Oh, Lee, your Sally's not in that league at all. She can't know what she's doing."

"I've got a feeling she does," Lee said, grimacing. "She thinks she's improving her chances in the Miss Tulipland contest. She wouldn't think beyond that. But if she keeps being seen with him, can you imagine the gossip?"

"Only too well. He has dated a few local girls, but most of his women are strangers."

"And he takes them to the Mill House? With his son there?"

"More often when Rikki's away visiting his mother. Even Lorens Van Der Haagen has *some* sense of decency. You'll have to have a straight talk with Sally. She always was hot-headed, I remember, but she must realize she's risking her reputation. People around here are a bit straightlaced, you know."

Lee, however, was sadly sure that if she attempted to interfere it would only make Sally more rebellious.

The following day, Lee had arranged a meeting with Peter Atkinson, manager of the local showplace of Springfields Gardens. Acres of flowerbeds, woods, and lakes extended behind wrought-iron gates and ticket booths. To one side were low-built offices, though on that day only a few gardeners were in evidence since the Gardens had not yet opened to the public.

A secretary greeted Lee and took her through to the office where the slim, bespectacled Peter Atkinson waited.

"It was very kind of you to spare me some time," Lee said as they shook hands. "I know you must be very busy."

"Yes, I am, but I was intrigued by your project," he replied. "Do sit down and tell me how I can help."

He talked with her for over an hour, showing her photographs and describing the year-round work entailed in a huge event like the flower parade, of which he was the organizer.

"It all started from very small beginnings," he said. "Years ago, people came just to look at the tulip fields in bloom, and the early Tulip Queens used to ride in a decorated bus to greet them. Then Adrianus Van Driel, who was involved with a flower parade in Holland, suggested building floats decorated with tulip heads. He designed the very first parade and the connection has continued. His son Kees is our designer now."

"Yes, I remember the excitement when Kees Van Driel married a local girl—she worked here at Springfields, didn't she?"

"Indeed she did. Anyway, Kees gets down to work on his designs as soon as the theme is chosen. And around November, the blacksmith—Geoff Dodds—starts to build the floats. You must go down and see him at work, though I'd be grateful if you don't take up too much of his time. He and Pete Bell—who does the strawing—are working all hours, seven days a week."

As, eventually, they left the boardroom, voices alerted them to the presence of another visitor in the secretary's office—a man who stared at Lee with a surprise that matched her own. He was dressed today in a formal business suit, but his hair curled as crisply as ever and his eyes held the faintly teasing smile which had come unbidden into her mind with alarming regularity ever since they met.

"Well, hello," Lorens Van Der Haagen greeted. "What are *you* doing here?"

"I came to do some research," Lee said. "And I really mustn't take up any more of Mr. Atkinson's time." Turning to the manager of Springfields, she shook his hand and thanked him warmly.

"Wait for me, will you?" Lorens Van Der Haagen suggested as she turned to the door. "I won't be a minute. Peter, I just wanted to have a word about . . ."

The two men moved out of the secretary's office and Lee exchanged a knowing glance with the young woman behind the desk.

"Taking a lot for granted, isn't he?" Lee said drily. "Thanks for your help. I may see you again."

"Oh, any time. I'm always here."

Outside, a pale sun lit the shrub-lined paths and neat beds which lay waiting for spring to waken leaves and flowers. There was an empty booth which advertised color slides, postcards, and souvenirs, and off to one side lay the restaurant complex.

Lee let herself out through the small unlocked gate in the entryway and saw Lorens Van Der Haagen's blue Jaguar parked behind her own Mini at the curb—just as it had been, briefly, down by the river. Judging by his request that she wait for him, he was not the type to stick to one woman at a time; he probably practiced his charm on every woman who crossed his path.

She had not really intended to wait, but she was still busy completing her notes when Lorens Van Der Haagen emerged from the office, strode through the gate, and leaned in the open window of her car.

"How about a coffee?"

"I just had one with Mr. Atkinson," she said. "Besides, I'm busy. I'm going to see the floats being made—if I can find the place."

"Don't you know the way? Then let me show you. I gather they're busy with our company's float at the moment. Perhaps we could have some lunch afterwards. I'm fascinated to hear about this book of yours—Peter told me about it. Perhaps I can help."

What a smooth worker he is, she thought. "That's very kind of you, Mr. Van Der Haagen, but—"

"It's Lorens," he said with a little pained frown. "I've told you that once."

"Lorens, then," she agreed. "Thank you."

"Good. Follow me. It isn't far."

Down a narrow back lane, the Jaguar turned into a yard surrounded by warehouses, and Lee saw her first example of a prepared float. It bore the twelve-foot-high figure of a cat, made of straw, with a big feathered hat, a walking cane, and huge cuffed boots. It stood casually in a corner of the yard.

Pulling in beside Lorens's car, Lee stepped out and stared admiringly at the float.

"Know who that is?" Lorens asked, coming to stand beside her.

"Puss In Boots, I'd guess. Mr. Atkinson said the theme was fairy tales. It's very clever, isn't it? He looks very pleased with himself."

"Yes, Geoff and Pete are craftsmen. Come and meet them."

In the vast cool spaces of the warehouse, several more floats stood in various stage of construction. On scaffolding, one man bound straw to the metal framework made by the blacksmith, who, with a mask over his face, was busy welding yet another piece of frame.

Lorens introduced Lee to the cheerful "strawman," Pete Bell, who said that he had learned the craft from his wife's uncle. He showed her the straw mats that were his raw material.

"They have to be brought from Belgium," he explained. "British straw doesn't work the same. This

39

is rye straw. I cut it to shape and then sew it with this big needle, see, and then clip it with these— they're old-fashioned sheep shears."

He was presently working on a huge, evil-looking figure with a spiky crown, behind what looked like a curving wall but was actually the back of an ornamental sleigh.

"This is the Haagen Bulbs float," Lorens said. "The Snow Queen. Look, here's the other half in metal, ready to be strawed."

The framework towered over him. On it, two husky dogs had been outlined in metal as they strained to pull the sleigh. Even in skeleton form, every detail was clear.

As the welding flame shut off, the blacksmith removed his mask and Lorens took Lee across to meet him. Dressed in coveralls, Geoff Dodds answered Lee's questions with quiet smiles. He showed her the cartoon-like designs painted by Kees Van Driel, and how they were converted to huge shapes with narrow strips of steel, all based around a rectangular framework that hid the tractor which powered each float.

A part from the various shapes he made, Geoff Dodds also had to work out the best places for seats for the riders and holders for flower arrangements which would add an extra touch of color to the floats.

Examining one of the very basic chairs built into the framework, Lee said, "They don't look very comfortable."

"The riders are usually too excited to notice," Lorens said, laughing. "The parade gets better every year."

"Well, Pete and I learn more about making floats every year," Geoff Dodds said.

"You're artists," Lee told him, but he demurred with another smile and a modest, "No, we're just craftsmen. But when you think of all the people who will be coming just to see the floats and the pretty girls who ride them, you like to think you've done your best."

"Which reminds me," Lorens put in, "we need another girl for the Haagen Bulbs float. Perhaps you'd like to be one of the Snow Queen's attendants. All you have to do is wave and smile."

Looking at the small, hard seat, Lee shook her head. "I'll be content to be a spectator, thank you. By the way, Mr. Dodds, do you know which float this year's Miss Tulipland is going to use?"

"She'll be the Fairy Queen," the blacksmith said. "That float's already gone down to the main warehouse, but you can go and have a look at it if you like."

"Thanks, I'll do that. Now I'll let you get back to work. Thank you for sparing me so much time."

"Oh, come again, any time," he offered. "It'll be a bad day when we can't spare five minutes for a chat."

By that time, Lee's notebook was full of facts and quotes.

"You wouldn't believe just two men could do all that," she said as she and Lorens came out from the chill gloom of the warehouse into the yard where the straw Puss In Boots grinned to himself.

"They do have occasional help," he said. "But I'd hate to think what might happen if one of them got sick. The tragedy is that after a few months all their work is dismantled. In October the straw is all

41

burned off, the framework cut down, and the whole process starts again. But you probably know that. Didn't you say you were brought up here?"

This reminder of their meeting in the woods brought Lee up short. For a while she had been so interested in the floats and the two skilled men who made them that she had forgotten the significance of the man beside her. He seemed so friendly and natural, but she must remember that he was also the "local playboy," the unfeeling brute who would seduce her silly cousin if he could.

"Yes, near here," she said, unwilling as yet to reveal her connection with Far Drove Farm. "Well, thank you for bringing me here. I expect I can find my own way back."

Smiling down at her, he slipped a hand beneath her arm. "You've forgotten we have a date for lunch. We both have to eat. Besides, I want to hear more about this book—and about you. You don't look like a writer."

"Why, what do writers look like?" Lee countered.

His smile widened. "I'm not sure. But I'm willing to bet that not many of them are as beautiful as you are."

He was too corny to be true, Lee thought cynically. He had it all down pat—the compliments and the ardent looks. If she hadn't known better, she might have thought he was really attracted to her. But then presumably that was what most of his women believed, poor fools.

"You still don't have to buy me lunch," she objected.

"I'm well aware I don't have to. I *want* to. What harm can it do? We'll be in public, right in the middle of town. I'm not likely to try anything you wouldn't approve of. Not in full view. Or have you got someone else to meet?"

If nothing else, he was persistent. Deciding that further argument would only make her look like a prim little scared rabbit, Lee gave in.

Three

They lunched at the best hotel, where the staff greeted Lorens with the cordial respect shown a frequent visitor. But if he thought this would impress Lee he was sadly mistaken. To her chagrin, however, he made a pleasant companion, conversing easily on several general subjects as they ate their meal. She found herself responding to his humor and kept having to remind herself that she was *not* supposed to be taken in by his all-too-obvious charms.

But it was difficult, for underneath the lightness of their verbal exchanges a current ran strong between them. His eyes said more than words about his pleasure in being with her, and though she knew it was all part of his technique she had to be constantly on guard against it.

He questioned her about the book she was planning, and about her work in the States.

"Are your parents still alive?" he asked.

"No," Lee said. "No, they're both dead, I'm sorry to say."

"I'm sorry, too," he said with what appeared to be genuine sympathy. "I know what a support parents can be. Which is why I worry about Rikki. I'm not sure a divided home's good for a child."

Since this was the first time he had alluded to his personal circumstances, Lee took the opportunity to ask frankly, "You mean you're divorced?"

Lorens looked surprised. "Of course I am. I thought you knew that. I'd hardly be asking young ladies to lunch if I were married."

"You might," Lee said.

He laughed, and the sound did odd things to the nerves along her spine. "Yes, I might, I suppose. How are you to know? But you're quite safe, Lee— my wife won't come chasing you. It's been a long time since she cared where I was, or who I was with, even before the divorce."

A variation of the "my wife doesn't understand me" ploy, she thought, and asked, "Were you married long?"

"Long enough," he said, and suddenly there were shadows in his eyes as if the memories were bitter. "Let's not talk about it. I'm more interested in you. How long are you planning to stay in this area?"

"I haven't any definite plans. Two or three months at least."

"All alone at the cottage?"

He was just too predictable for words, she decided. "I'm not alone. I have my work. Besides, I'm used to being on my own. I enjoy solitude."

"Surely not all the time? You need to go out and enjoy yourself occasionally."

"I have friends here," Lee said, "Mrs. Weaver's granddaughter, for one. I've an open invitation to visit her any time."

"It doesn't sound very exciting," Lorens objected. "Would you let me take you out some time? Rikki will be going to his mother for the Easter holidays, so I'll be at loose ends, too."

He talked as if his son were his sole interest outside business. What a liar the man was!

"Oh, I wouldn't want to put you to any trouble," she murmured.

"It's no trouble. Believe me, Lee." Ardent green eyes smiled as he leaned across the table and took her hand in his. "I know what it's like to be lonely. But . . . perhaps you're right. I'm going too fast. We'll talk about it another time." Releasing her hand, he signaled the waiter and smiled at Lee apologetically. "I'm afraid I must get back to the office. But thank you for your company. It's been a long time since I enjoyed a meal so much—and I don't mean because of the food."

"I enjoyed it, too," Lee said. "Thank you."

"And if I can be of any help—if you want to know about bulb growing or anything—you'll give me a call, won't you?" He produced a business card, jotted down an extra few digits on it, and gave it to her. "That's my private number, at the Mill House."

He did not press her for another date, or imply that he expected some return for the expense he had gone to in giving her lunch. Outside the hotel he simply bade her goodbye, said he looked forward to seeing her again, and strode off to his car.

He was, of course, an old hand at this game of seduction. He had sensed her reticence and decided not to push too hard, not yet. But she had no doubt she would be seeing him very soon. He knew exactly where to find her.

But she found herself regretting that it had to be this way, both of them playing cat and mouse, because in many ways Lorens was the most attractive man she had ever met. If he had been what he seemed to be . . .

But that, of course, was just the sort of wishful thinking that drew other women into his net. He *was not* what he seemed. She must be careful to remember that.

She had been at the cottage almost a week, but she had not yet learned to ignore the cheerful din of the dawn chorus, which woke her very early each morning. Even that Sunday, when she had planned to sleep in for a while, the loud twittering from the woods brought her out of her dreams as the first strokes of sunlight lifted above the horizon. Groaning, Lee turned over and pulled the blankets over her ears, but the merry birds seemed to have congregated right outside her window.

Then in among the birdcalls she seemed to hear another sound—a cry that had human origins. Curious, she leapt out of bed and went to open the window wider.

"Help!" a thin voice wailed. "Oh, help me!" A boy's voice. Rikki!

"Hang on!" Lee yelled at the tangle of bushes and trees along the wood's edge, where the voice seemed to be coming from. "Hang on, I'm coming!"

Hastily scrambling into some clothes, she ran out into the lane where the rising sun shone full in her eyes, brightening the world and tipping tiny new leaves with gold. A slight mist lay over the fields, cloaking the world in dew.

"Rikki!" she shouted as she ran, scanning the woods for signs of the boy.

"Here!" the wail came back to her, not far away now.

She plunged into the first pathway that opened from the lane—a pathway bearing a sign saying *Strictly Private*—and found herself among a maze of trees where morning shadows stretched.

47

"Keep shouting!" she called. "Where are you?"

She found him eventually, sprawled in a muddy ditch half full of water, amid a tangle of rusty barbed wire that was caught in a growth of weeds and nettles. The barbs had snared him much as the thorns had snared her a few days before, but this was much more serious. Rikki was trying not show his fright and distress, but he was shivering and there was blood on his clothes.

Extricating him proved to be a tricky business, forcing Lee to get down into the muddy water herself. Barb by slow barb she untangled the wire from his clothes, speaking to him reassuringly, and eventually the bedraggled pair climbed free.

"Can you walk?" Lee asked, not liking the look of a jagged wound that poured blood from the child's hand. "The important thing is to get you clean as soon as possible."

Since the Mill House was a lengthy walk away through winding paths, she took Rikki back to the cottage, stripped off his clothes despite his protests and put him into a warm bath. She took care to clean the nasty cut on his hand and the deep bleeding scratches on his legs.

Soon Rikki was wrapped in a towel, green eyes huge and woebegone in his pale face. How like his father he was! Stoically, he allowed her to clean his wounds with antiseptic, and put a dressing over the worst one in the cushion of his right palm.

"How on earth did you manage to fall into that ditch?" she asked, kneeling to attend to the scratches on his legs as he sat on a kitchen stool.

"I thought I'd seen a willow-warbler," he said dully. "I wasn't looking where I was going. Now I've *really* lost my binoculars. Dad'll be furious."

48

"I imagine he'll be too pleased to have you safe home to worry about anything else," Lee said. "Rikki, dry your hair before you catch cold. Did your father know you were out so early?"

From the stubborn look that answered this question, she guessed that he had sneaked out without anyone's knowing.

She sat back on her heels, sighing. "Oh, Rikki! You mustn't do things like that. What if I hadn't heard you? You might have been there for hours."

"And I suppose you'll tell him," he said, thrusting his bottom lip out sulkily.

"I'll have to. You know that."

Not for the first time, she regretted that there was no phone at the cottage. She couldn't call Lorens to set his mind at rest, but since it was still early perhaps he didn't yet know that Rikki was missing.

Briskly, she towel-dried the boy's fair hair, lent him her slippers, and then fetched a blanket to wrap him in before returning upstairs to change her own wet, muddied clothes.

The mist was rising across the fields as she drove up to the winding main road and crossed the bridge. The road followed the curve of the river, where the Mill House stood impressive, its old wheel silent now beside a footbridge where willows bent.

A tall hedge gave privacy to the front garden, which was mostly lawn with a broad graveled area for cars. Crocuses made a colorful carpet, in beds backed by the drooping branches of yet more willows. The house itself was white with black trim, the main door boasting a shiny brass knocker. The place was silent, its curtains still drawn across tall windows.

Holding Rikki's undamaged hand, Lee led the blanket-draped child across the gravel to the door, where she pressed a bell and waited, trying to shield the boy from the cold breeze. After a few moments the door was opened by a gray-haired woman dressed in black skirt and cardigan with a pink blouse.

"Oh, my Lord!" she groaned. "What's he been up to now? Mr. Lorens! Mr. Lorens!" She moved away, to the foot of a flight of stairs where a gleaming banister snaked up to a dimly lit landing.

"Come on," Lee murmured consolingly to the boy, leading him into the hall and closing the door.

A gold-colored carpet spread across the floor and up the stairs, while the walls were adorned with advertising mirrors and posters, twenties-style.

Mrs. Rufford—as Lee later learned was the housekeeper's name—was by now halfway up the stairs, still shouting for Mr. Lorens. Eventually, an ill-tempered, "All right, I'm coming," answered her.

Face grim, Mrs. Rufford came down to the hall, giving the boy a sharp look. "I'll let your father deal with this, you young villain!" With which she disappeared into regions at the back of the house.

Clutching Lee's hand, Rikki lifted an anxious face. "You won't let him be angry, will you? I didn't mean any harm. But I couldn't sleep and the birds were singing . . ."

"Yes, I know," Lee said softly, laying a comforting arm across his shoulders. She stoked the still-damp hair from his forehead, then looked up as she sensed another presence.

Lorens had obviously been roused from sleep. His hair stood on end and his only garment was a silk robe of midnight blue. Seeing the tableau in the hall, he sighed heavily and came down the stairs, jaw set and his eyes fixed on his son, who quailed against Lee.

"Now what?" Lorens asked heavily.

"Don't be angry," Lee pleaded. "He's hurt. He fell into a ditch and got all tangled up in some barbed wire. I've done what I can to clean him up, but perhaps you ought to call a doctor just to make sure."

Lorens's eyes met hers in sudden understanding and the silent message passed between them: danger of tetanus. "I'll do that," he said. "Go and get some clothes on, Rikki. And bring the blanket back for Miss Summerfield."

At once the boy dodged away, thumping up the stairs awkwardly with Lee's slippers loose on his feet.

"I've got his clothes in a plastic bag in the car," Lee said. "They're filthy, I'm afraid."

"He always gets filthy in the woods," Lorens replied grimly, watching his son disappear. "If I've told him once I've told him a hundred times. He was out birdwatching, I suppose."

"He said the dawn chorus disturbed him. It does that to me, too."

For the first time he gave her his full attention, and as always Lee was disconcerted by the expression in his eyes as his anger faded. "How am I going to thank you?"

She managed a breathy laugh. "There's no need. I'm repaying a favor. You untangled me a few days ago."

"I hadn't forgotten," he said, his gaze caressing her face. "At least the scratch has healed. But you've got a smear of mud on your cheek."

Throwing up a hand, she rubbed at the caked roughness. "I'm afraid I didn't bother with mirrors. There wasn't time."

"I'm not complaining," he said, smiling down at her as he ruefully explored the stubble on his own jaw. "I'm not fit to be seen myself."

That wasn't true, she thought. Coming straight from sleep he looked disheveled, a little vulnerable, but the dark robe only made her more aware of broad shoulders, lithe muscles, and skin that would feel warm and smooth to her touch.

She caught her breath, clenching her hands against the thought of touching him. How many women had seen him like this, how many had awakened beside him warm and languorous after a night of love? Was the black-haired woman upstairs at this very moment? And would Sally be next?

"The least I can do is offer you a cup of coffee," he said. "Wait in the sitting room while I get dressed, will you?" He turned aside and opened a door, showing her the shadowed interior of a room carpeted in the same gold as the hall.

"Oh—no. No, I really mustn't stay," Lee said, and was relieved when Rikki reappeared, fully dressed now and carrying the blanket over one arm, with her slippers clutched in his hand. "It's awfully kind of you, but—"

"But you've got someone waiting for you, is that it?" Lorens asked, an edge in his voice.

Her eyes swung back to his face, but it was a moment before she realized what he was suggesting. "No!" she gasped. "Certainly not. But you've got to have breakfast and I really think Rikki ought to see a doctor without any delay. Besides, I . . . I'm going out later. I have to get ready."

"Then I won't detain you."

The boy approached Lee, eyes anxious as he handed her the blanket and slippers. "I'm sorry if I was a nuisance," he said. "Thank you very much for helping me."

"You're very welcome," Lee replied with a smile, unable to resist touching his thin shoulder. "I hope you'll soon feel better. Just take more care in the future. And if you're over by the cottage, come and see me."

He regarded her wonderingly. "May I?"

"Of course. I'll be glad to see you." Glancing at Lorens, she found him watching her sardonically. "I'll just bring his clothes in for you."

"Thank you," he said. "Rikki, go and get your breakfast. And try not to get into any more scrapes before I get there."

" 'Bye," Rikki said to Lee before trudging away.

Lee turned to open the door and stepped out into sunlight slanting across the front graden. Her shoes crunched on the gravel as she made for her car, where she tossed the blanket and slippers onto the back seat before removing the plastic bag heavy with Rikki's mud-soaked clothes. As she turned, she was surprised to see that Lorens had followed her out, his hands deep in the big pockets of the robe to prevent it from flying open in the breeze. She was unnervingly aware that beneath that blue silk he was naked.

"I hope you won't be too hard on him," she said, unable to meet his eyes. "He had a bad fright. It might have taught him a lesson."

"Let's hope so. Oh, are these his things? Thank you. What became of his binoculars?"

"They must still be in the woods. I'll look for them."

"No please don't bother. I'll get him to show me where it happened. We've given you enough trouble already. I'm grateful, Lee."

Laughing nervously, she tossed her dark hair and forced herself to look at him. "Think nothing of it. You'd better not stay out here. You'll catch a chill. It's not very warm to be standing about in next to nothing."

He gave her a wicked grin that said he was aware of her awareness. "No, it's not," he agreed. "Well, 'bye for now. And thank you again."

He was still standing there as she drove away. She could see him in the mirror as she waited at the gate until a line of motorbikes had gone by on the main road.

After lunch, she set out for Far Drove Farm and tea with her family. She had used a minimum of makeup and wore a cream turtleneck under a cherry-colored suit. That afternoon she had two goals in mind: to claim the belongings her grandmother had left her, and to find out just how deeply Sally was involved with Lorens Van Der Haagen. The first should be simple, but the second promised to be more of a problem.

As she drew up in the yard outside the farm, her uncle came out to meet her, his stocky form clad in gray flannels and a maroon blazer with the badge of the local darts club on the breast.

"I expected to find you still here the other day," he said with a questioning look. "What did you go and rent a cottage for? We've room here. It's your home, isn't it?"

"I'm afraid I've got used to being independent," Lee said.

Her aunt, looking uncomfortably formal in a blue wool dress and high heels, waited in the front room, the "special occasion" room with its heavy curtains across the windows and hanging plants that shut out even more light. Forest green drapes hung at the windows and also on a rail behind the door, to keep out drafts, and the walls were covered in a heavy red-figured paper which seemed to make the room claustrophobic.

For a while they made stilted conversation. Bert and Jinnie asked about her life in America. To them New York was a place filled with muggers and rapists; they could not understand how anyone could enjoy living and working there.

"Isn't Sally at home?" Lee asked eventually.

"Oh, she's gone riding," her aunt said. "She'll be in later. She was sorry not to be here, but Lady Sue needs exercising."

"She's probably gone over to Highdyke to see Neil," Uncle Bert added. "They're courting, you know."

"Yes, so Aunt Jinnie said," Lee replied. "I met Neil the other day. He says Sally's in the finals of the Miss Tulipland competition this year."

Her aunt became more animated. "She's in the last twelve. They'll be picking the top six at a meeting next Wednesday, and of course the Ball's on Friday. They'll announce the winner then. We shall have to see if we can get you a ticket, Lee. You could sit with us, couldn't she, Bert? I'm sure Sally's got a good chance of winning. She's certainly the prettiest, and she's got a good lively personality."

The awkwardness of the conversation was almost unbearable, Lee thought. They were as uncomfortable making this false small-talk as she was.

"I'll make us a cup of tea," her aunt said, getting to her feet.

Left alone with her uncle, Lee stared at the flames of the gas fire, aware of a clock ticking swiftly on the mantel. Bert shifted in his chair, cleared his throat.

"The daffs have done well this year," he said. "We've just brought the last lot into the greenhouses. We're a bit late with them. Any day now, the outdoor ones will be through."

He was happiest talking about what he knew best—raising daffodil and tulip bulbs. Lee let him ramble on while she made what replies seemed necessary, and after a while Jinnie returned with a laden tray.

"By the way," Lee said as spoons tinkled in the best china, "you mentioned a keepsake that Gran left for me. What is it?"

Her aunt and uncle exchanged a look, then Jinnie forced a smile. "Why, she left you the Georgian silver tea set. I've been keeping it for you. I didn't want to risk mailing it—it might have got lost. I'll clean it up for you before you take it. Unless you'd like to leave it here for safe-keeping?"

"No, I'd like to have it," Lee said. "Not that I need anything as a reminder, but if she wanted me to have it I'll be glad of a memento. Don't worry if it's tarnished. I can clean it myself."

"You want me to get it now?" her aunt asked in consternation.

"There's no hurry," Lee said. "We'll find it before I leave."

"What, today?" Jinnie demanded.

"If you don't mind."

Her aunt stood up, indignation sharpening her features. "If you don't trust us, I'll go and find it right now. No—stay where you are. I'll get it, even if I do have to move a whole load of stuff." She stormed from the room and slammed the door, leaving the green velvet curtain trembling.

"She doesn't mean anything," Bert said quietly. "You know what she's like. Of course you're entitled to have the tea set. We're all a bit edgy, Lee. Having you suddenly come back like this has been a surprise. And you've changed. Hardened."

"I've had to," Lee said.

In an apparent effort to entertain her, Bert took her out to show her the greenhouses where tray after tray of daffodils lifted green buds, some of them already opening to show the promise of yellow trumpets.

"We'll have to get this lot cut tomorrow," her uncle said.

The routine was familiar to Lee, who had grown up with it and done her share of the backbreaking work of cutting daffodils and tulips in the fields. Other bulbs, for forcing early bloom, were planted in trays of peat during August and left under straw until Bert had the first batch brought into the warmth of the greenhouses. He usually sold his first crop around Christmas. From then on until a brief period in June, a bulb grower's life was hectic.

Bert grew daffodils, narcissus, and tulips, along with other flowers and vegetables to make full use of his greenhouses off-season. In the fields, since bulbs could not be grown in the same soil more than once every four years, he also grew crops of potatoes, sugar beets, and wheat.

"I'll cut you a bunch of daffs before you go," he said as they emerged into an area where used bulbs, still in their drying peat trays, lay upside down among straw. When dry, the bulbs would be sterilized and sorted, some to go on the market and others to be replanted in the fields and in more peat trays for next year.

Several cats prowled around, on watch for the mice and rats which could decimate the bulbs, and as Lee watched the slender felines, a clop of hooves made her glance up.

Leading a gray mare, Sally came through from the main yard. She gave Lee a brief, polite smile, though her eyes remained wary. She was shorter than Lee, boyishly slim in jeans and sweater with her pale hair streaming from beneath a riding hat.

"Well," Bert said heartily. "I'll leave you two girls to talk. I'll tell your mother you're back, Sally." Seeming glad to be released from duty, he shuffled hurriedly away.

"So this is Lady Sue," Lee remarked, rubbing the mare's nose. "She's lovely. How are you, Sally?"

"Better in health than temper," Sally said shortly, jerking the horse toward a brick barn. "You might have told us you were coming back. I couldn't believe it when Mum said you'd just turned up out of the blue."

Inside the barn, light came from a window festooned with cobwebs. Riding tack hung on the wall beside a pile of straw, and a stall had been built of new wood.

"Are you annoyed because I came back?" Lee asked.

Sally bent to unbuckle the horse's girths. "It's got nothing to do with you. I've just been to Highdyke. Neil and I had words."

"About what?"

"Oh . . . nothing, really. He makes me so mad at times." Heaving the saddle from the mare's back, Sally dumped it on a trestle and began to unfasten the harness. One of the cats prowled in among the shadows.

Lee perched next to the saddle, watching her cousin deal with the mare. "I gather you and Neil are—"

"Are what?" Sally snapped. "What's mother been saying? Honestly! I wish people would mind their own business. *I* might have other ideas. Neil's so slow."

"Slow?" Lee queried. "In what way?"

"In every way! I'm really fed up with him, Lee. Anyway, he's not the only fish in the sea, whatever Mum thinks. I may surprise them all yet. I've got my eye on someone a lot more exciting than Neil Clayton."

Just as Lee had feared. "Oh? Anyone I know?"

Sally glanced over her shoulder, looking Lee up and down assessingly. "I doubt it. Anyway, why should I tell *you*? You'd only start giving me unwanted advice. You always did. Just because you're a whole three years older you always thought you knew best."

"I was only trying to help. Okay, I promise not to play big sister ever again. But don't expect Neil to wait around forever while you're busy making a bad name for yourself."

Catching her breath, Sally swung around, narrowed eyes darting fury. "What do you know about it? Neil's *told* you, hasn't he? He said he'd seen you the other day, but he didn't tell me you'd both been gossiping! So what did he say—that I'm seeing

Lorens Van Der Haagen? Well, so I am. And what's more he's interested. Very interested. A woman can tell that sort of thing. *And* he lives at the Mill House—that place you and Gail always used to say you'd own some day. Well, maybe for once I'll get in first. Maybe *I'll* be mistress of the Mill House. How will you like that?"

"I can't imagine why you think you're in competition with me," Lee said stiffly. "But Lorens Van Der Haagen is no shining white knight. He's divorced. He has a son. And I doubt very much that he's looking for another wife. Don't do anything you'll regret, Sally. You're out of your depth with that man."

"You mind your own business!" Sally yelled.

Lee stood up. "I certainly will. That's that's the last word I'll say on the subject. If you're intent on ruining your life then go ahead. I expect there are a dozen girls who'd be glad to marry a decent, hard-working man like Neil Clayton."

Suddenly, Sally burst into tears, her arms along the horse's back as she sobbed and moaned.

"Sally . . ." Worriedly, Lee went to touch her cousin's shoulder. "Sally, don't. What is it? You haven't already got in too deep, have you?"

Whirling around, her arm slapping Lee away from her, Sally revealed a tear-streaked, contorted face. "Leave me alone!"

"Oh, I wish we could be friends!" Lee said passionately. "Why won't you talk to me calmly? Perhaps I could help."

"I don't want your help!" Sally raged. "I hate you. I just hate you, Lee. You've always been there ahead of me. Oh, why did you have to come back?"

"I'm beginning to wonder that myself," Lee said quietly and, turning on her heel, walked out into the fresh air.

Four

Sally took a very long time over bathing and getting changed, while Lee and her uncle had more desultory small-talk in the front room and her aunt laid the dining room table for tea. Jinnie had refused Lee's offer of help.

Eventually, after being called at least five times, a sulky Sally came to join the family for tea—a massive ham with salad and pickles, followed by home-preserved fruit with cream, and cake. Every remark addressed to Sally met with a snappy answer and consequently the mood was hardly congenial.

Lee made excuses to leave as soon as the meal was over. No one tried to detain her. In the kitchen, she was given the silver set of teapot, milk pitcher, and sugar bowl in huffy silence; then as if on an afterthought Jinnie produced a large lacquered box.

"This is Gran's jewelry. She left you that as well. Just take care of it, now."

"Yes, I will," Lee said. "Thank you. And thank you very much for tea. It was delicious. I'll . . . see you again."

"Yes, love," her uncle said. "Drop in any time. You're always welcome. I don't know what's been wrong with Sally, but—"

"She had words with Neil," Jinnie said. "She told me so when she came in."

Altogether it was the most miserable afternoon Lee had spent in ages, probably since she left the farm five years before.

She drove home very fast, eager to put Far Drove as swiftly behind as possible. In the quiet Sunday evening streets of Spalding church bells pealed tunefully, and along the steep banks of the river daffodil leaves promised color to come. The town's peacefulness soothed Lee's agitation. What did it matter, after all? She really should have known that five years' absence would not help her relationship with her family. And if Uncle Bert had forgotten the daffodils he had promised, at least she had come away with what was important—the tea set and the jewelry which were her grandmother's last gift.

At the cottage, she looked through the contents of the lacquered box, finding a mixture of costume jewelry that was largely worthless but for its sentimental value. A couple of pieces appealed to her—a pair of dangly jet earrings and a brooch with a tawny stone of polished quartz at its center. She remembered her grandmother wearing a good many of the items, and they brought back bittersweet memories.

Sometimes, feeling unloved and unwanted, she had shut herself in her room and cried. And each time her grandmother had come to stroke her hair and croon over her until the child Lee had grown calmer. She had never been able to explain what was wrong, but the old lady had seemed to understand.

Who was there now to understand how bitterly hurt she felt? She kept remembering Sally's red, contorted face. *I hate you, Lee. I just hate you.* But why did Sally hate her so?

A sharp knock on the door made her look up, wondering who the caller could be. There was no car outside except her own. Combing her hair roughly with her fingers, Lee went into the narrow hall, opened the door, and found a smiling Lorens Van Der Haagen on the porch.

After a moment, she wondered why she should be surprised. This was the next obvious move in a seducer's campaign.

"I saw your car was back," he said. "I hope I'm not interrupting anything. I just thought you might like to know about Rikki."

A good excuse, she thought as she stepped back. "Come in. Yes, how is Rikki? Did you take him to see a doctor?"

"I took him to the hospital," Lorens said as she closed the door and evening shadows gathered around them. "They cleaned him up again and gave him a tetanus shot, but you'd done a good job. Since he's running around as usual, I expect there's no real damage done."

"I'm glad to hear it," she replied.

"Oh—and I did find his binoculars again, though I'll have to see about getting that ditch cleaned out. It's dangerous the way it is."

"Yes, it certainly is," she said, disconcerted by his nearness in the narrow space. "Please . . . come into the living room. It's dark in this hall."

Lorens followed her and looked curiously at the assortment of jewelry scattered across the velour cloth that protected the table. Beside it stood the tarnished tea set.

"Have you been poking in the antique shops?" he asked with amusement.

63

"No." Hastily, Lee began to put the jewelry away, embarrassed to have him see these personal things. "They were my grandmother's. She left them to me when she died. I've just been to collect them. Will you sit down?"

He remained standing, close beside her. "Did she die recently?"

"No. It's more than two years. My aunt's been keeping these things for me."

"I didn't realize you still had relatives here."

Arms clasped around the smooth black box, Lee gave him a bleak smile. "We don't get on very well, I'm afraid. Just one of those things. Please . . . sit down. I'd offer you a drink, but I haven't got anything in the cottage. Would you like a cup of tea, or coffee?"

"Nothing, thank you," he said, but the expression in his eyes said a great deal more.

To her dismay, Lee realized she was glad of his company. And if he kept looking at her like that she would throw herself into his arms and pour out all her troubles. But her deepest hurts were not for Lorens Van Der Haagen's knowing. She faced him, still clutching the box like a shield, wanting to get past him.

"You're something of a lady of mystery, aren't you?" he said with a smile.

"Am I?"

"Oh, yes. But I like mysteries." His smile widened. "Am I in your way? Sorry. Yes, thank you, I'll sit down."

Her taut nerves eased a little as he put space between them and took a seat on the small couch by the fire.

64

"I'll just put these things away," she said, gathering up the tea set. "Excuse me a minute."

She hurried up the stairs and dropped her burdens on the bed before pausing to run a comb through her hair and check her makeup. After a moment she realized what she was doing. Making herself presentable? For Lorens Van Der Haagen? Good grief!

Then a wicked idea occurred to her, making her stare at her reflection in shocked amazement. Lorens was attracted to her, wasn't he? Of course, he would be attracted to any lone female who seemed ripe for his purposes, but that wasn't the point. He thought her unaware of his reputation. She had, for the moment, taken his mind off Sally.

Suppose she pretended to be falling for his advances? Suppose she pretended to be responding? Perhaps if Sally knew that he was also making a play for Lee it might bring the silly girl to her senses.

It would mean taking a risk, but it might be worth it. Was she capable of carrying it off?

Returning to the living room, she found Lorens kneeling by the hearth transferring coal from the big brass bucket to the fire by means of a pair of tongs. He sat back on his heels, gesturing with the tongs.

"I hope you don't mind. The fire was about to go out."

"No, that's fine," Lee said brightly. "Make yourself at home."

It was that time of evening when the sky remains light but indoors gray shadows deepen. She wondered if she should put the light on and draw the curtains, but decided to leave it for a while. Twilight could add its own intimacy to this encounter.

She sat down on the couch, watching Lorens add pieces of coal to the glow with careful precision.

"I love an open fire, don't you?" he said. "The Mill House is centrally heated, but occasionally I have a fire in the main room, just to add to the ambience."

"Yes, it's pleasant," Lee agreed.

Through lowered lashes, she considered his broad back. He wore a soft gray sweater over a dark blue shirt, with matching blue slacks. Even kneeling by the fire he gave an impression of contained power. Fair hair curled around his ears and his neck, softening the line of his cheek and strong jaw.

He was very clever, behaving casually and naturally to give her a false sense of security, she thought. But any minute now he could come and sit beside her.

He sat back on his heels, glancing over his shoulder to smile at her. "That should do the trick. We'll soon have a good blaze going. It's been a nice day, but the evenings still turn chilly."

"How typically English," Lee laughed, "to talk about the weather."

He took the cue, as she had expected. Rising lithely from the rug he slid onto the couch beside her, his thigh barely inches from hers as he smiled into her eyes. "What would you prefer me to talk about?"

"Anything you like."

His green glance ran over her face and rested on her mouth, and Lee's skin reacted by producing a million tingles. No wonder women fell for him, she thought. One ardent look from him was enough.

"I think I owe you an apology," he said in a low voice. "This morning, when I implied you might have someone waiting here for you . . . I don't know what made me say it. I suppose I wanted to know if—if there's someone in your life."

He was still watching her mouth, making her head reel as if she were drunk. Nervousness made her tongue flick out to wet her lips, and she cleared her throat, though her voice still came out husky.

"There isn't."

His lashes flickered and suddenly she was drowning in green eyes flecked with gold, eyes that said he desired her. "No one? Not even in the States?"

"No," she managed. "No one special."

"You know why I'm asking?"

There ought to have been some reply to that—something coy or clever—but for the life of her she couldn't think what to say. Her mind had gone blank. She felt as if she were adrift on a fathomless lake of sparkling green water, knowing she would have to go under.

She closed her eyes, unable to bear the hypnotic power of him, and she felt his breath warm on her mouth in the sweet, agonizing moment before his lips touched hers very softly, moving to murmur her name in a way that spoke more to her heart than her ears.

She swayed toward him, her hands against the softness of his sweater as his arms came round her, holding her gently, and he kissed her with infinite tenderness. Then a hand behind her head pressed her to lean on his shoulder. He drew her more closely against him, sitting relaxed with her curled at his side.

67

Through a mist, Lee watched tiny yellow flames dance in the fire, while beneath her cheek the soft wool rose and fell with his breathing and she heard his heart beat an accelerated rhythm.

"What about you?" she murmured.

"Me?" A hand stroked the hair from her temple and he let his lips rest there a moment. "How do you mean?"

"Is there someone in *your* life?"

"There is now."

She lifted her head to look up at him. "No, really, Lorens. Tell me the truth."

"It is the truth," he said in a low voice, with every appearance of sincerity. "Until a few days ago, when I met you, my life was empty."

A quiver of disgust ran through her as she tucked her head back onto his chest. *Liar. Cheat!* What about the other women—especially that raven-haired beauty she had glimpsed with him in the woods? What about Sally? Lee had actually seen him kiss Sally.

"Do you know what first attracted me?" he asked.

"No? What?"

"Your sense of humor. Another woman, caught in an embarrassing situation the way you were in that thornbush, might have been angry, or burst into tears. *You* laughed."

The room was thick with twilight now, lit only by the flicker of the fire. One of his hands lay against her face, his fingers playing in her hair, but the other hand, on the arm that curled around her, had somehow contrived to arrive where his thumb could caress the side of her breast. The touch was slow, absent-minded, as though he were not aware of it. But he knew, all right. He knew too much about the

68

subtle ways of arousing a woman, expecially one he believed to be unsuspecting.

And unfortunately Lee was all female. Her mind might know him for what he was, but her physical self could not help responding. She lay with her arm across him. He was warm, strong, comfortable to lean on, and beneath her ear the sensuous beat of his heart had a soothing effect. But all her senses were alert to the caress of that thumb and the hand that slowly moulded itself to the underside of her breast.

Shocked by her own reactions of pleasure, Lee pushed herself upright, making his arm loosen from around her. Flicking at her hair, she smiled at him.

"How about that coffee now?"

"I wish I could," he said, lifting a hand to straighten her hair and letting his fingers trace the curve of her cheek. "But I have to get home. Rikki won't go to bed unless I make him. Mrs. Rufford says she has no control over him."

"Mrs. Rufford, the woman I met this morning? She's your housekeeper, isn't she?"

"Yes. Her husband looks after the garden and does general maintenance. They've got rooms of their own at the back of the house. But . . ." Sighing heavily, he stood up. "But Rikki's *my* responsibility. So I must go, I'm afraid."

He held out his hand, drawing her to her feet. Then he slid his arms around her waist and laid his forehead on hers, looking into her eyes.

"Thank you, Lee. Thank you for a few minutes of perfect peace."

"You're very welcome," she murmured, and let her hands slip up his chest, then clasped them behind his neck as he bent to kiss her.

His mouth moved on hers softly, asking questions that her instinct answered, and as her lips parted his arms tightened about her, pulling her against his body. His kiss demanded a response she could not deny as his tongue explored further. Her arms fastened around his neck, holding him to her, one hand tangled in the soft gold of his hair, and all the time he pressed her closer. Even through their clothes Lee felt the ripple of his muscles against her body, and then his hand moved to the base of her spine, forcing her nearer.

She laid her hands on his face, then on his shoulders, pushing him away. "No! Pleases, Lorens—"

His hips withdrew, putting space between them, and in the fire's glow he smiled at her with darkened eyes. "It's all right," he murmured. "It's all right, Lee. Don't be afraid. I can be patient." He laid soft kisses over her face, his lips touching her cheeks, her eyes, and finally her mouth again as gentle as a sigh. "I must go," he said in a deep undertone. "I'd suggest that I might come back later, but that might not be wise. Besides, I've got work to do."

As he released her, she stepped back, bewildered by the strange force that had almost swept her away on its tide. "Work?"

"Yes." A wry grimace crossed his face. "I've got to get my papers in order for a board meeting. I fly to Amsterdam tomorrow."

"Oh?" Breathlessness made her sound dismayed, and Lorens caught her hand, drawing her in beside him.

"Only for a few days. I'll be back on Friday. How would you like to go to the Tulip Ball with me?"

Trying to make her brain work properly, she blinked at him and said stupidly. "Can you get tickets?"

"I've already got them," he informed her. "I'm supposed to be one of the judges." He began to lead her toward the front door, out into the near-dark hall. "This business trip means I'll miss the final judging session on Wednesday, so all that remains is an appearance at the Ball. Will you come?"

She could hardly see him in the shadows, but his hand remained firm around hers and she sensed his tall strength only inches away. Her thoughts darted illogically. Sally would be at the Ball—and Uncle Bert and Aunt Jinnie. To be with Lorens . . . what scandal! What excitement!

She heard herself say, "Yes, I'd love to," and then she was in his arms again, his mouth hot and sweet on hers and his body hard, pressing against her in silent confirmation that he wanted her.

He wrenched himself away, breathing fast and heavily in the darkness. "I'd better go. I'll see you on Friday. Take care, Lee."

"You too," she managed.

There was a brief glimpse of dying daylight, a cold draft, then the door closed and she was alone. She leaned weakly on the wall, her head spinning, her body still on fire from his assault on her senses. Stupidly, all she could think was that she would not see him again for five days.

No! That was a trap she must avoid. Physically he was devastating, but it was only physical. Being a grown woman, fully equipped for lovemaking, she could hardly hope to remain unmoved by a man's closeness, but that was all it was. Her head and her heart must remain aloof.

Shaking herself, she returned to stare at the fire in the dusk that cloaked the sitting room. She had known the risks when she began this campaign. Now he would be eager for a repeat engagement, for a chance to try further intimacies. That was what she wanted, wasn't it?

She knelt on the rug, watching flames leap among the coal. This was where he had knelt, and talked about the ambience of a fire. If only he didn't play the part so well! He knew exactly how to appeal to her emotions: *Is there someone? My life was empty until I met you.*

Of course, he couldn't know that she had been forewarned by Gail, or that she knew of his involvement with Sally. As far as he was concerned, Lee was a newcomer and ignorant of his real character. He also must have sensed that she was not the sort of woman to slip easily into bed with every man she met. So he was playing it carefully, one step at a time.

Oh, she knew very well what he was up to! Why, then, did she feel so despondent? Because the dreamer inside her actually wanted to believe him? That was crazy.

Even though he was far away, Lorens haunted her. Memories of his presence filled the cottage and even when she was out she was constantly reminded of him every time she glimpsed a fair-haired stranger, or when one of the big Haagen Bulbs trucks rumbled by. He even came vividly into her dreams, where she allowed him liberties that made her wake in a sweat.

There was, too, his son.

Rikki arrived on the very first evening, when Lee was busy cleaning the silver tea set.

"You did say I could come," he reminded her.

"Yes, I remember," Lee said, pleased. "It's good to see you, Rikki. Come on in. How's your hand?"

He showed her the grubby dressing and recounted his experiences at the hospital, chattering naturally and happily.

Lee took him to the kitchen, where he asked if he could help with the silver. Putting a plastic bag over his injured hand, so as not to further blacken the dressing, Lee demonstrated the use of the polish and Rikki set to work on the sugar bowl.

"Dad's gone away," he informed her. "I hate it when he's away. It's so boring with just Mrs. Rufford. I wanted to go with him, but he wouldn't let me miss school."

"I should think not," Lee said. "Besides, he'll be busy. Won't you have a holiday soon, anyway?"

"Yes," Rikki said gloomily. "Then I'll have to go to mother's again. She'll drag me around the zoo, and the parks, and the museums. I expect there'll be another new uncle around as well."

Lee found him watching her with a most unchildlike expression of world-weariness. She guessed that his "uncles" were his mother's male friends, and that Rikki understood the situation only too well.

"You're lucky your mother takes you out to nice places," she said.

"But I've seen them all before! I hate London. It's boring. And after a few days she'll get tired of taking me out and send me to play with the children across the road. She always does. And when I don't want to go she'll buy me something to keep me quiet." Lifting the sugar bowl, he squinted at the bright patch he had cleaned. "Is this worth a lot of money?"

"Yes, I think so. Be careful with it. It's very special. It belonged to my grandmother."

Interested, Rikki began to talk about his own grandparents, who lived in Holland. He apparently enjoyed his visits to them. Lee was relieved to have gotten past the sticky subject of his mother, though she wondered if Lorens knew the sort of conditions his son lived under in London.

When she decided it was time for Rikki to go home, he didn't want to go. He said he was too tired to walk back through the woods and anyway it would soon be dark; so Lee took him back to the Mill House in her car. She felt sorry for the poor child when the gruff Mrs. Rufford threatened to box his ears and report to his father if he didn't behave.

After that, Rikki turned up at the cottage every evening. He seemed lonely without Lorens, and Lee began to believe that, whatever his faults, Lorens was not a bad father.

She worried frequently about the Tulip Ball. Had she been too hasty in accepting Lorens's invitation? What would her family think when she arrived with him? It was best not to anticipate, she decided. Best to play it by instinct as it happened.

If it happened. Friday evening arrived without word from Lorens.

Rikki did not come that evening; he had said he would stay at home to be with his father. Wondering if Lorens had been delayed in Amsterdam, or if he would arrive ready dressed for the Ball, Lee began to prepare herself, washing her hair and taking a bath in the tiny extension off the kitchen.

Still dripping, wrapped in a terrycloth robe, she was towel-drying her hair when someone rapped a tattoo on the front door. Lee froze, guessing who the visitor would be. Then after a moment the impatient knocking came again, followed by the rattle of the latch.

"Lee?" Lorens's voice came down the hall. He was actually inside the cottage!

"Just a minute!" she called, hastily folding the robe more securely and cinching the belt before fastening the towel turban-like around her head.

Red-faced, she hurried into the hall. "Really, Lorens—"

"Tulips from Amsterdam!" he declared as, with a magician's gesture, he produced from behind his back the largest bunch of tight-budded tulips she had ever seen. The buds were still green, giving no hint of their color.

"And why the devil don't you have a phone?" he demanded. "I tried to call you from Holland. When they said they couldn't find a number I cursed them for inefficiency, but now I discover there isn't a phone at all! What was I supposed to do—send postcards that wouldn't arrive until after I was home again?"

He stood there, tall and fair in his business suit, half laughing and half exasperated as the words poured out of him. His presence filled the cottage with life, and Lee's response of relief and pleasure dismayed her.

He laid the tulips on the hall stand before advancing to her with arms outstretched. "Come here, you lovely woman," he said as he wrapped her in a tight embrace. "I've missed you. Have you been behaving

75

yourself? Not swept off your feet by some muddy marshman?"

"I—" Lee began, but the words died against his mouth as he kissed her hungrily, hard arms flattening her against him. As before, she was drawn at once into the sensuous delight of his nearness, but this time a part of her managed to remain detached and watch his technique from a distance. Flowers— yes, naturally—and talk of phone calls he would have made had he been able; and then the hint of jealousy . . .

"You smell delicious," he muttered, nibbling her ear and throat. "You're all warm and damp. I could devour you."

"Lorens—" Lee protested, but he lifted his head and claimed her mouth again as if she were a banquet and he starving. Her stomach jolted. The towel unwrapped from her hair and fell unheeded to the floor. She wrapped her arms around his neck and kissed him back.

His hands began an exploration of her spine as if assuring himself that she was naked beneath the thick robe. His fingers spread over her rib cage and stroked down to her waist and farther, to curve around her buttocks and bring her close to him.

Then, abruptly, his hold eased and he removed his body from hers, looking down at her with bright desire. "Unhand me, woman. There's no time for this now."

Lee smiled mistily up at him, her fingers flirting in the curls near his ears. "It was your idea, not mine."

"Meaning you object?" he asked, laughing. "I know better than that. And what do you expect when you greet me dressed like this? I'm only human."

"You shouldn't have walked into my house," she retorted.

He let her go, giving her a mock frown. "Be thankful it was only me and not some burglar. You ought to lock your door, you know. Seriously—a woman on her own has to be careful, even around here."

"So I've just discovered," Lee said archly.

"I'm tempted," he replied, narrowed eyes not disguising his amusement, "to make you pay for that, but it will have to wait. I'll pick you up at seventhirty. Okay?"

"I'll be waiting. And thank you for the flowers."

Lorens glanced to where the tulips lay. "They're special. The only ones in England at the moment. Which reminds me—you know I mentioned we need another girl for the Snow Queen float?"

"Yes, I remember."

"Well, will you do it? Please, Lee. It might be fun. And you could look after Rikki for me. He's going to be Kai—you know, the boy the Snow Queen carried off?"

It was almost emotional blackmail, but she rather fancied the idea of being involved in the flower parade. "All right, if you're desperate, I'll do it."

"Thanks, angel," Lorens said, and kissed her again. "See you later."

He left as abruptly as he had come, leaving Lee feeling as though a whirlwind had stormed through the cottage. Scoundrel he might be, but like most scoundrels he could be utterly charming when he tried. Was there any wonder that, down through the ages, women had made idiots of themselves over men like him? Of course he seemed plausible. That was the nature of the beast.

Returning to the kitchen, she set the tulips—three dozen of them—in a bucket of water to have a drink overnight. He must have been joking when he said they were special, since millions of tulips were presently on sale, or growing in greenhouses, or waiting to flower in the fields. Still, it had been nice of him to bring them, whatever his motives.

Later, with her hair making a shining dark frame for her oval face, Lee stepped into a dress of soft pinks and greens, carefully drawing the bodice to cup her bare breasts before fastening the long zipper and straightening the spaghetti straps. With a glance at her watch, she slipped a topcoat on for warmth, and as she went down the stairs a horn tooted from outside.

Lorens opened the Jaguar's door as she appeared and she paused to admire the sight he made in immaculate evening dress, smiling and fair beside the shining car.

"Did you lock up properly?" he asked as she slid into the car.

"Yes, I did."

"Are you sure?"

"I'm positive. Don't fuss. I'm used to taking care of myself."

Closing the car door, he strode around to the driver's side and climbed behind the wheel, smiling at her. "You look lovely. I'll be the envy of every man at the Ball tonight."

Lee sighed to herself, saying, "You're awfully corny."

"I know." He slanted a grin at her as the Jaguar moved smoothly down the lane. "But has it never occurred to you that clichés only become clichés because they're the most concise way of expressing something? In the future, though, I'll try to be more original. Have you been to the Tulip Ball before?"

"No, never."

"Didn't you ever enter the competition yourself?"

"Hardly. It's not my style. But . . ." She hesitated, thinking that sooner or later he would have to know of her connection with Sally. "As a matter of fact, my cousin's one of the contestants this year."

He shot her an astonished look. "Your cousin? Does she look like you?"

"Not a bit."

Lorens frowned to himself, watching the road. "Which one is she, then? Describe her to me."

"Oh, she's . . . small, ash blonde. Her name's Sally Freeman."

Since she was watching for it, she saw the way his frown bit deeper for a moment before he gave her a sidelong glance. "You're Bert Freeman's niece?"

"Why, yes. Do you know him?"

"I do business with him, on occasion. I didn't know . . . Of course, I'm not that closely acquainted with the Freemans, but I don't remember them mentioning you."

"Why should they? I've been away for five years. Anyway, what about Sally's chances? Will she win?"

"She may. I wasn't there at the meeting on Wednesday, so I don't know what the final decision was."

At least Sally's flirting could have had no influence on the results of the contest, for which Lee was relieved. But she still had little idea of how Lorens felt about Sally.

Very soon the Jaguar slid to a halt in the middle of Spalding, by the South Holland Center where the Ball was to be held. People in evening dress laughed as they went up the steps to the portico of the building. Somewhere among them would be her family, with Sally feeling tense and excited as she awaited the results of the competition. Half the town would be there to see it. And half the town would also be waiting to see which young woman Lorens Van Der Haagen had chosen as his partner for the Tulip Ball. Why on earth had she agreed to come? Was she mad?

Five

Among the throng of women in the cloakroom, Lee saw no one she knew. She checked her coat, inspected her makeup, and went out into the stream of hairdos and fancy dresses. Near the door into the ballroom, Lorens stood amid a swirl of people; he was talking to a slender woman who had her back to Lee, but even so Lee thought she recognized the waterfall of raven hair that cascaded over a blue gown. She was about to meet the woman who had come looking for Lorens in the woods.

For a moment she watched as Lorens laughed with the woman, then he looked across and caught Lee's eye, beckoning her to come to him. His gaze swept over her as she approached, and when he met her eyes again her heart twisted at the possessiveness of his smile.

He claimed her hand, drawing her close to his side. "Let me introduce Rosa Gunthorpe—she's a local councilor, and another of the judges. Rosa, this is Lee Summerfield."

"Nice to meet you," the woman said, smiling as she shook Lee's hand.

Rosa was not at all what she had seemed from a distance. She was older, for one thing, with an odd strand of gray in that fine black hair, and by no means was she a beauty; her features were too large and her teeth crooked.

Then a portly man with smooth gray hair joined them and was introduced as Rosa's husband, John Gunthorpe.

"I've claimed us a table," he said. "As far from the stage as possible. I don't want to get deafened by the music."

In the ballroom a band played from the stage, lights glittered, and people laughed and chatted among glorious flower arrangements where tulips held pride of place. Around the floor, tables of varying sizes accommodated the parties who were gathering. Lee was somewhat relieved when John Gunthorpe led his party to a corner of the room where the lights were a little less bright. She searched the throng for sign of her family, but could not see them.

She did, however, unexpectedly catch the eye of Gail's mother. Mrs. Weaver looked surprised, started to wave from across the room—and stopped with her mouth open when she saw who Lee was with.

"You look gorgeous," Lorens breathed in her ear, his arm around her waist, drawing her nearer to a chair.

Well aware that Mrs. Weaver would report all of it to Gail, Lee shot him a quick smile and took her seat, facing away from the dance floor where a few couples were beginning to glide to the music. Lorens and John went off to get drinks, while Rosa sighed with satisfaction and leaned on the table.

"I always enjoy this evening. It's usually great fun. Have you known Lorens long?"

"No," Lee said, biting back a temptation to add *Have you?* From their attitude to each other, Rosa and Lorens were old friends—John, too. Since Lorens had his pick of younger, prettier women, surely not even he would conduct an affair with the wife of a friend?

"The judging's been very difficult this year," Rosa chatted. "More entries than usual, for some reason. Of course, the first heat is fairly easy. You can tell at a glance that some of the girls are too nervous ever to carry it off—Miss Tulipland has a full program of duties throughout the year. And some of them only enter for a joke. Usually one stands out, but this year there are two or three very likely girls."

Lee was hardly listening; she was watching her family arrive, with Neil Clayton looking uncomfortable in a suit and tie. Sally looked wonderful, her ash blond hair flowing straight and shining to her shoulders. Her white silk dress had a skimpy top and a skirt that draped against her thighs with every movement.

"That's one of our contestants," Rosa said, following her gaze. "Lovely, isn't she?"

"Yes, she is." Realizing that her family were too busy finding seats to notice her, Lee looked at the woman opposite her. "She's my cousin, actually."

"Ah," Rosa said with a grin. "Then I won't say any more. I didn't realize you were a local girl."

"Oh, I'm not—not any more. I've just come back for a couple of months to do some research, for a book about the Tulip Festival."

That topic occupied them even after the men returned. Both John and Rosa had been closely involved with the parade for several years and had many stories to tell, to which Lorens added his share. Around them the Ball got under way and Lee began to relax, except that she knew the moment must come when Sally saw her.

That was the reason she had come, of course—to show Sally that Lorens was fickle. But now, much too late, she saw her actions in another light: Sally would think that Lee had deliberately set out to take Lorens away from her, out of pique and jealousy. That was the way Sally's mind worked; she would blame Lee, not Lorens. Oh, God! Why hadn't she thought of that before?

Then Lorens laid his warm hand over hers, making her look at him to see him smiling with that special look in his eyes. "Shall we?" he asked, nodding at the floor where the crowd had thinned after an energetic disco session. The band had swung into a fox trot.

Putting on a smile to disguise her inner panic, she nodded.

On the edge of the floor, he took her in his arms and began to lead her through the basic steps. Lee felt sick, as if she might faint. The room seemed to sway, a murmur of voices underlying the music, as she kept her eyes fixed on Lorens's white shirt.

"The Freemans are here," he said.

"Yes, I know."

"They look surprised. Didn't you tell them you'd be here?"

Not looking at him, she shook her head.

He drew her closer. "Relax, Lee. Let yourself go." A few more steps took them near the band, away from the area where her family sat, and other couples moved in between.

"What's wrong?" Lorens asked softly.

"Nothing." Taking a deep breath, she smiled up into his anxious eyes. "Nothing at all."

His frown said he didn't believe her, but he laid his cheek on her hair and his arms were suddenly tender, comforting her. Lee closed her eyes, trying to forget about what people would be saying. Dancing with Lorens was a marvelous experience.

Everything would be so wonderful if only the rest of the world would go away; if only he were sincere; if only Sally would understand. If only . . . If only . . .

She felt unreal, as if the Ball were a nightmare from which she would soon wake. But she couldn't wake. She was trapped there, having to pretend, to laugh and talk and be sociable.

"It's time for us to make a move," Rosa remarked to Lorens as a few people began to leave the ballroom.

"Right." He stood up, pausing to smile at Lee. "I'll be back just as soon as I can."

The final six competitors for the Miss Tulipland title were due to join the judging panel in another room. Lee saw Sally rise from her place, speak briefly to her parents and Neil, and make for the door. Across the room their eyes met, Sally's cold and hostile as she tossed her pale hair and walked on, the white silk dress flowing about her legs.

"Now for the big announcemnt," John said. "Would you believe it—even I don't know who's won? Rosa wouldn't tell me. Would you excuse me for a while? I want to have a word with someone."

"Yes, of course," Lee said, and stared down into her glass wishing she had the courage to run away.

A moment later, someone sat down in the chair Lorens had vacated and she lifted heavy eyes to see Neil Clayton's round face frowning at her.

"What are you doing with the Gunthorpes? Couldn't you have come with us? I'd have got you a ticket."

Lee almost laughed. When the Freemans arrived, she had been alone with Rosa. Presumably they thought she had been brought by Rosa and John, and Lorens had simply joined them. How ironic!

"Aunt Jinnie did say something about getting a ticket," she said, "but I heard no more about it."

"It's a pity the Gunthorpes are so friendly with Van Der Haagen," Neil said grimly. "Watch him Lee. He's a smooth operator. I wish you'd come with us instead."

Should she say that she was Lorens's guest, not Rosa's? The situation had become ludicrous. She still wanted to laugh, but if she had she might have wept, so tangled were her nerves.

Lights dimmed as the music ended and the dancers returned to their seats. An MC took up a microphone while the eight judges, six men and two women, filed in. As excitement mounted, the six finalists paraded down the length of the ballroom, all of them young and slender in pastel gowns: blondes, brunettes, and one redhead—just the way Lorens liked them, Lee thought bitterly.

He stood with the other judges, hands clasped in front of him as he smiled at the parade of pretty girls. He was the youngest of the judges, also the tallest and by far the best-looking, his fair hair gleaming in the bright lights that illuminated the show. Watching him, Lee felt misery well up inside her.

"Wish her luck," Neil said, taking her hand where it lay on the table.

She glanced at him and saw that all his mind was with Sally, who looked both demure and sexy in her clinging white gown.

The chairman of the judges stepped up to the microphone and spoke of the difficulties of the decision and the beauty of all the contestants; then at long last he announced the runner-up—the girl who would be deputy to Miss Tulipland that year. She was the pert redhead wearing green.

As the girl stepped forward to claim her silver tray and the cloak which went with her office, Neil squeezed Lee's hand so hard she almost cried out. He grinned at her and, under the noise of applause, said, "It's got to be Sally. Don't you think so?"

"I hope so," she said, meaning it. The title would mean a lot to her cousin, and obviously Sally's winning meant a lot to Neil, too.

"Ladies and gentlemen!" The chairman's voice boomed over the speakers. An eager hush fell over the room and five sets of families and friends crossed their fingers and beamed at their own contestant.

"Ladies and gentlemen . . . This year's Miss Tulipland is . . ." A roll on the drums, and then—"Sally Freeman!"

Lee saw Sally clap her hands to her face as the crowd erupted into applause. The new tulip queen came forward to have her sash and tiara fitted, along with a pale blue cloak, and then everyone in the ballroom stood up, clapping and shouting in appreciation.

Caught up in the excitement her cousin must be feeling, Lee too stood up to be able to see better. Neil grabbed her and, to her astonishment, planted a kiss on her cheek, hardly knowing what to do with himself. Lee had never seen him so animated.

The new Miss Tulipland and her deputy paraded around the edge of the dance floor to take their applause with smiles and blushes. Beneath a glitter of diamante, Sally's eyes were filled with tears. She did not acknowledge Lee or Neil, though Lee knew she had seen them.

And only then did Lee notice that Sally was wearing around her neck a choker made of turquoise chunks—their grandmother's necklace, which the old lady had shown with pride but seldom dared to wear. Until that moment, Lee had forgotten all about it. Now she felt as though she could hardly breathe.

"I'd better get back," Neil said. "We'll all be going to supper—the contestants and their families, and the judges. Are you going with the Gunthorpes?"

She looked at him blankly, still shocked and hurt by the sight of that vivid choker, which by rights should have been with the rest of her grandmother's jewelry in the lacquered box.

"What?" she said. "Oh . . . I don't know."

"Well, I'll see you later, anyway."

Lee sat down again, twirling her glass on the table. After a while John returned, explaining that he had got trapped when the ceremony began, and then a laughing Rosa reclaimed her seat.

"I was dying to tell you, Lee, but I just couldn't. Sally will be a great asset to the town this year. Apart from being very pretty, she gets on so well with people. She just claimed Lorens for a dance—she said he was the only one of the judges who hadn't got a wife to object."

Lee laughed, as she was expected to, but she sought out Lorens and Sally among the couples now circling the floor. The Miss Tulipland tiara glittered as Sally threw back her head and laughed up into her partner's smiling face before sending a triumphant sidelong glance straight at Lee.

A great tidal wave of rage mounted so fiercely in Lee that she had to ask to be excused. Knowing that Rosa and John were surprised by her abrupt departure, she fled to the ladies' room.

Ignoring the few other women who were there, she splashed cold water onto her burning face and used a paper towel to pat herself dry. Her reflection stared back at her from the mirror, wide dark eyes in a face that was ghastly pale except for two ugly splotches of color on her cheeks. All she could think about was Sally wearing Grandmother Freemán's most cherished necklace, and with Lorens's arms around her.

She closed her eyes tightly, fists against her forehead. Then abruptly a gasp of laughter shook out of her and as she bit her lip tears welled hot and uncontrollable in her eyes.

This was the last straw, the final insult from the Freemans. They had stolen that necklace. Stolen it!

"Are you all right, dear?" a kindly voice said from beside her. "Shall I fetch someone? Who are you with?"

All Lee's muscles tensed as she forced herself to outward calmness. "No, it's all right. I'm fine. Really. But thank you for offering."

The elderly woman smiled at her. "That's all right, dear. I was your age myself once. But nothing's as bad as it seems."

That, thought Lee, was exactly what her grandmother might have said. Oh, Lord, she mustn't cry any more!

Her face was a wreck. She doused it in more cold water and made repairs to her makeup, planning to escape, maybe find a taxi. One thing was sure—she couldn't go back in that ballroom and face all those people.

Eventually, the procession of women in and out of the cloakroom eased temporarily. Lee got her coat, slipped it on, and hurried for the exit, only to stop short at the sight of Lorens waiting for her.

"What's going on?" he asked in astonishment. "You're surely not leaving? Lee—have you been crying?"

"Don't ask," she muttered, averting her face. "And don't try to stop me, please. I should never have come. You go and have your supper. I'll find my own way home."

She tried to slip past him, but he caught hold of her, bending to try to see her face. "What's this all about? Can't you tell me? What on earth happened?"

"Nothing happened!" The fierce lie hissed out of her as she lifted her head and looked at him with tear-flecked eyes. He looked bewildered, concerned.

But it was hardly the place for an emotional scene, with people in and out all the time.

Lorens's expression changed as he straightened. "I'll take you home. We can't talk here."

"You can't leave!" Lee said desperately. "You'll be missed. No one will notice if I go."

"Of course they will. I'll notice. Look, either you stay with me, or I come with you. There's no other choice, Lee. I'm not letting you go home alone in this state. Wait here. I'll just go and tell John and Rosa that we're leaving."

As soon as he was out of sight, Lee ran down the stairs and through the foyer. Drops of rain blew in the wind as she peered along the street in vain hope of finding a cruising taxi. But in Spalding taxis did not drive around waiting for a fare; they came in answer to a phone call.

Oh, God! she thought, lifting her face so that the wind cooled her skin. What a hysterical scene she was making. Calm, cool, together Lee Summerfield, who had planned to seduce a seducer. And why? To punish the Freemans? To save Sally? Sally would do as she pleased, and her parents didn't give a hoot about Lee.

It was laughable. Lee hadn't even caused the shock-horror she had expected, because her family hadn't realized she was with Lorens. Well, they would realize now, when she disappeared from the Ball with him.

A shudder ran through her as she leaned on one of the brick pillars of the grand entrance to the Center. Her arrogance had got her nowhere, made no difference to anything, except to herself.

Hurried footsteps made her glance up as Lorens erupted through the door and stopped, breathing heavily. "I thought you'd run out on me."

"I almost did," Lee said dully. "If this had been New York, I'd have hopped in a taxi and been long gone."

"And I," said Lorens, "would have come after you." He raised the collar of her coat, holding it up to her face as he leaned to press his lips to her forehead. "Let's get in the car. You're cold."

With an arm tucked warmly around her, he led her to the Jaguar and settled her into the passenger seat with gentle care.

"Okay?"

She raised a wan smile. "Yes, fine."

When he was in the driver's seat he did not start the engine at once but sat with an arm behind her, a finger brushing her cheek. "Tell me about it."

"There's nothing to tell," Lee said. "I didn't feel very well, that's all. I'm sorry to have ruined your evening."

"You haven't." For a moment he watched her profile in the darkness, then with a sigh turned to the wheel and flicked the engine into life. "I don't know why you're lying to me, Lee, but I'm going to find out."

He left her to think over this threat as he drove through the town and out into the countryside beyond.

"It's something to do with the Freemans," he said eventually. "Don't deny it, Lee. You've been like a cat on hot bricks all evening. You couldn't even bear to look at them. Now, why?"

Letting out a heavy sigh, Lee slid down in the seat as more tears stung her sore eyes. "I can't tell you."

"You said you didn't get on very well with them," he recalled. "Is it some family feud? They're not bad people, you know. Bert's a bit set in his ways, and his wife's inclined to be sharp, but I find them easy enough to get on with."

"And Sally?" Lee asked hoarsely.

"Sally's no different from any other girl her age. Maybe a bit high-strung, but . . . This surely isn't all because I danced with Sally, is it? You can't be that possessive."

"No, of course I'm not!" she snapped. "That has nothing to do with it." But even as she spoke she knew she lied. Watching him dance with Sally *had*

92

hurt her, because it reminded her of that other time when, on a windy riverbank, he had held Sally in his arms and kissed her passionately.

Will you stop pretending to care about me? she wanted to yell at him.

"Then what is it?" he asked.

Abruptly, she twisted her head to look at him in the dim light from the dashboard. "It's got nothing to do with you, Lorens. Mind your own business!"

His answer was a swift glance and a tightening of his lips, though he said nothing. Neither of them spoke again until the car eased to a halt outside the cottage.

Switching off the engine, Lorens turned to face her, saying quietly, "I know you're upset, Lee, but I'm about out of patience. You're behaving like a spoiled child. Go home now. Get some sleep. We'll talk about this tomorrow."

She drew a deep, shuddering breath and shook her head. "We won't, Lorens. I don't want to see you again."

"Oh?" His voice was ominously quiet and controlled. "Am I allowed to ask why?"

"I'm not obliged to give you reasons."

"That's true. Very well, if that's the way you feel, perhaps you'll get out of my car and let me go back to the Ball. There are plenty of women there who *will* want to see me."

"I'll just bet there are!" she flung at him, and scrambled from the car, slamming the door.

Before she reached the gate, he shot away with a squeal of tires, red taillights dwindling down the straight, dark lane.

Lee ran for the cottage, fumbled with the key and let herself into the dark hall. She leaned on the door, head back and eyes closed, her thoughts fuzzy with distress. Now, at last, Lorens had shown his true colors. He had gone to find someone else—probably Sally. And Sally would be high tonight, on triumph and unaccustomed alcohol. She might be reckless enough to leave her parents and go with Lorens to some secret place where. . .

Wrenching herself upright, she told herself she didn't care. If Sally got hurt it would be her own fault, and there would be kind, gentle Neil waiting to pick up the pieces. Sally wouldn't lose out in the long run; too many people cared about her.

And no one cared about Lee.

She shook herself, disgusted by her own self-pity, and made her way down the dark hall into the sitting room, where a faint red glow showed from the banked-down fire. She sank onto the couch, head in hands, thinking how astonished her New York friends would be to see her. Lee Summerfield was the tough one, the independent woman who came smiling through life's knocks to forge on with a career that promised to be brilliant.

That was who she was—a strong, self-confident career woman, not the lonely little orphan brought up so begrudgingly at Far Drove Farm.

She put herself to bed, but for the first time she was conscious of the loneliness of the cottage. Wind sighed through the woods and an owl called somewhere nearby. There were squeaks and rustlings, and then an increasing patter of rain on the window.

Imagining the bright lights back at the Ball, she had a vivid picture of Lorens holding Sally, his dark tuxedo contrasting with her white gown, his fair head bent near her ash blond one as they smiled into each other's eyes. A quiver of emotion ran through her and she turned over, buried her face in the pillow, and wept bitterly, more lonely than she had ever been in her life.

Part of her had believed that Lorens would come back.

By morning she felt calmer, coldly determined to do what she had to do. Her uncle had accused her of hardness and it was true that she had grown a shell around her inner pains. Last night she had allowed that shell to crack, but now it was patched up again. She would go to the farm and *demand* that they return the turquoise necklace.

Having showered and dressed, she made herself some breakfast, trying to ignore the tulips which still stood in a bucket in the corner of the kitchen. They were too sharp a reminder of things she wished to forget.

Even so, when she thought about the way Lorens had breezed in, laughing and talking a mile a minute, and the way he had kissed her, as if he really had missed her . . . Oh, no! If he had meant any of it he wouldn't have gone back to the Ball; he wouldn't have left her alone.

Leaving the cottage exactly as it was, all untidy with the curtains still closed and the fire dead, she went out to her car, climbed in and turned the key. Nothing happened. Further attempts at starting the engine only met with the same result. She got out to peer at the engine, which looked fine to her, not that she was any kind of mechanic. Slamming the hood shut, she glanced around irritably, seeing no sign of human life but a distant tractor crawling along a field. Seagulls cried overhead and in the woods the birds were doing their usual thing, but there was no one around to help with a stubborn engine.

Frustrated, Lee kicked the tire, which released a few of her pent-up feelings. Now the darn car had given up on her. Why had she ever come back to this rural backwater? There wasn't even a phone!

"So all right," she lectured herself. "You get to a phone. Come on, you independent woman, get yourself out of this one."

There was, of course, a phone at the Mill House, but no way was she going to the Mill House. What, make it look as if she were chasing that unfeeling brute? No, thank you.

She returned to her bedroom to change into flat walking shoes, and then having locked the cottage securely, she set out to walk down the lane and along the main road to where she seemed to remember seeing a red phone box, down a little cul-de-sac where a group of houses stood.

It was much farther than she had thought, and to her irritation she was passed by one of the local green buses, which might have stopped for her if she had thought to flag it down in time. She reached the phone box eventually, called a taxi, and then had to wait twenty more minutes until the car arrived.

Streams of Saturday morning traffic crawled through Spalding, with shoppers crowding the pavements. By that time, the daffodils on the steep banks by the river were out, nodding their yellow heads in the sunlight. A green haze was spreading through trees and gardens as leaves unfurled. Lee was reminded that the following weekend would be Easter, when Springfields Gardens would open to the public and the floral glories of spring and summer would burgeon.

It was a lovely time of year. Perhaps it had been worth coming back just to see an English spring again.

The taxi proved to be expensive, so rather than ask the driver to wait she paid him off at the entrance to the farm. Then, taking a deep breath, she marched across the yard and knocked on the door.

She was answered by a low 'woof' from Jed. Was the family out, she wondered, or sleeping late after the Ball?

Eventually, just as she hammered for a third time, she heard Sally's voice say, "All right, I hear you, I'm coming."

From the looks of her, Sally had just got out of bed, still bleary-eyed and with a flounced robe clutched around her, her hair trailing across her face. She stared at Lee through pale blond strands.

"Good morning," Lee said evenly. "I'm sorry to get you out of bed, but I've come for—"

"Oh, you didn't," Sally broke in, shivering a little. "I had to get up to answer the phone. You'd better call him back. He was looking for you."

"Who was?" said Lee, perplexed.

"Lorens Van Der Haagen! Who else? You've really got your hooks into him, haven't you?"

Six

"Lorens phoned here, asking for me?" Lee said blankly. "What did he want?"

"He didn't say." Holding her wrapper under her chin, Sally shuddered. "You'd better come in. That wind's cold. I don't want to catch my death just when I've become Miss Tulipland. Mum and Dad are both out in the greenhouses cutting tulips. There's a rush on. Make yourself some coffee, if you like. I'll just go and get some clothes on."

Alone in the kitchen, Lee opened cupboards and found everything where it had always been; Aunt Jinnie was a methodical housekeeper. But this was not the way Lee had planned her visit. She had meant to march in and demand to have the necklace returned. What did Lorens mean by phoning the farm?

The kettle was boiling by the time Sally returned wearing pink pants and a blue sweater. In her hand she held the bright turquoise choker, which she offered to Lee.

"This is yours," she said, a stubborn set to her mouth. "I borrowed it for the Ball. I know I should have asked, but . . . I had it in my room. I'd been trying it on with my dress. When Mum gave you the jewel box she didn't realize this was missing, and when she found out . . . well, we thought you wouldn't mind."

"Of course I don't mind," Lee said. What else could she say?

Sally looked at the stones trailing from her hand. "It is pretty, isn't it? It looked so nice with my white dress."

"Yes, it did. You looked marvelous. Congratulations, by the way." On impulse, she added, "Keep the necklace, Sally. I'd like you to have it."

Sally's head came up, a look of amazement on her face. Lee saw her cousin's blue eyes gleam and knew she would love to accept the offer, but not when it came from Lee. Sally wanted nothing from Lee.

"No, I couldn't. It's yours." She thrust the necklace into Lee's hand and turned away. "I had my share from Gran's estate. She left me some money. That's how I got Lady Sue. Do you still take your coffee light?"

"Yes, please." Sadly, Lee tucked the turquoises away in her bag.

Having made the coffee, Sally brought it to the table and sat down, gesturing Lee into a chair opposite. "And what was the matter with you last night? You left rather suddenly. Mum and Dad were a bit upset that you didn't even come and say hello to them. You *were* with Lorens Van Der Haagen, weren't you?"

Lee tried to read the expression on her cousin's face but couldn't see beyond the bright challenge in Sally's eyes. "Yes, I was."

"I thought so. Mum said you must have come with the Gunthorpes, but from what Lorens said I gathered otherwise. Neil was quite worried. He seemed to think you were in some sort of moral danger."

"Well, I assure you I'm not," Lee replied. "I've more sense than to let myself get seduced just for fun."

"That," Sally said grimly, "is exactly what I thought. Well, you're not going to get away with it, Lee. Not this time."

The glittering, daggers look that went with this speech took Lee aback. She stared at her cousin. "Look, Sally—"

"I don't want to hear your excuses!" Sally hissed, leaping to her feet. "I just want you to know that I've got claws, too, and I'll use them if I have to. You've had one chance. You're not getting another." She made for the outer door, swung it open. "I'm going to the stable. Don't come after me. Phone the Mill House if you want—a lot of good it'll do you!"

Lee finished her coffee, stunned by the exchange with Sally. Eventually, with no sign of anyone returning to the house, she set out to walk the three long miles back into town. What was the point of phoning the Mill House? The charade with Lorens was over, for her.

She passed fields where daffodils grew in long yellow rows and women bent to cut the last few budded blooms for market. The rest would be allowed to die, to feed the bulbs which were the real crop, and soon outdoor tulips would demand attention.

Walking at a brisk but steady pace, Lee watched the spires of Spalding grow taller against a backdrop of blue sky, with bands of cloud looking like mountains on the horizon. It was a beautiful sunny day full of April promise and if only her heart had been lighter she might have enjoyed the walk.

At least she knew she had tried—tried to extend the hand of friendship and tried to help Sally. What more could a person do? Neil Clayton ought to be doing something if he wanted to win Sally, instead of waiting patiently for her to come to her senses. *He makes me so mad,* Sally had said, and Lee could understand that. Of course Sally found Lorens more exciting. What woman wouldn't?

She had been trying not to think about Lorens, but now memories came back sharp and painful— Lorens laughing, Lorens tender, dancing with her in the ballroom, holding her close and warm in the firelight. A bittersweet yearning filled her, but she fought it back, knowing that to Lorens the whole thing had been a game. He hadn't meant any of it. But how easily a woman could fool herself into believing a man like that.

Carrying two plastic bags full of groceries, Lee shouldered her way out of yet another crowded store onto pavements cramped with pedestrians.

"Lee!" a female voice hailed her and here came Gail, herself burdened with loaded baskets. "Hello. How are you?"

"Fine, thanks," Lee said shortly. "You?"

"Weary," Gail sighed. "Phew! I usually do my shopping on a Friday, but Jamie wasn't very well yesterday. You look a bit peaky yourself. Heavy night?"

"I didn't sleep with Lorens Van Der Haagen, if that's what you mean," Lee snapped.

Gail stared at her, astonished as much by her tone as her words. "What's wrong with you? Why should I think—"

"I'm sorry," Lee said, sighing. "I'm in a foul mood. I assumed your mother would have told you I was at the Tulip Ball with Lorens."

"Were you?" Beneath her red curls, Gail's eyes grew round. "No, I haven't spoken to Mum today. How on earth did that happen?"

"Oh, I had some crazy idea about showing Sally what sort of man he is. It all went wrong, of course. I had a row with Lorens and he went off in a huff. Then this morning my car wouldn't start and I had to trail out to the farm by taxi, and I had another row with Sally, and then I walked back, and—"

"Hold it," Gail broke in briskly. "You're coming with me. Jim's coming to pick me up in a few minutes. We're having fish and chips for lunch, then he's going to a football game. Jamie will be having his nap, and you can tell me all about it in peace and quiet."

Gail had everything well-organized. Her life might be a simple one, but at least she knew who she was and where she was going. Just being with the Forrester family helped Lee unwind from the tension that had claimed her.

Later, at the bungalow, with Jim gone to his game and little Jamie peacefully asleep, Lee sat with Gail in the cozy living room and poured out the whole sorry story. She didn't go into the more intimate details of her encounters with Lorens, however, or reveal that there had been times when she had been tempted to put aside her doubts and believe in him. With Gail, she adopted a scornful tone when she spoke of Lorens.

"He's so obvious. You know—making out like I'm the only woman in his life and all the usual rubbish."

"And how far has it gone?" Gail asked.

"It hasn't gone anywhere. He's kissed me a couple of times, but that's all."

"I don't know how you can," Gail said with a shudder of distaste. "He's just using you, Lee."

"He *is* very attractive," Lee argued. "In fact, if you hadn't warned me about him before I met him—"

"I'm glad I did! Oh, I know you probably think I'm hopelessly old-fashioned, but believe me it's worth waiting. I was glad there hadn't been anyone before Jim. It will be the same for you, when you find the right man."

A wry smile crossed Lee's face. "Is there such a being? Sometimes I wonder."

"Of course there is. You may meet him tomorrow. Or he may be waiting in New York. Lee . . . let Sally do as she pleases. You've tried to help and it didn't work. Stay away from Lorens Van Der Haagen. You're not as tough as you pretend."

Lee knew this was good advice, but since Lorens had been phoning around looking for her she doubted very much that it was all over. A man like that was used to having women fall at his feet; he wouldn't like to be led on and then dropped. Inadvertently, Lee had probably only succeeded in making him more anxious to conquer her.

She stayed for tea with the Forresters, then Jim took her home and had a look at her car. He said there was something wrong with the starter motor and that he would come by in the morning to fix it. Lee was not to worry; he would soon have her mobile again.

"What would I do without you and Gail?" Lee said. "Thanks, Jim."

"What are friends for?" he returned, and departed back to his wife and son.

Lee had dumped her groceries in the hall in her eagerness not to keep Jim away from home too long. Now she carried the bags into the kitchen, and stopped in alarm when she saw the broken window, with cardboard taped across it. From the inside!

A creepy feeling feathered down her spine. Someone had been in the cottage in her absence—someone who had no right to be there. She wished that big Jim Forrester had stayed a few minutes longer, for the cottage suddenly felt unsafe.

Then she notice the piece of paper on the table, with a note scribbled on it.

"Lee," the note read. "I'm sorry about the damage but I was afraid something had happened to you. When you get back, please let me know you're safe. Please!" The final please was underlined heavily three times, and it was signed, "Lorens."

What on earth did he mean? Had he broken into the cottage imagining he might find her lifeless? Oh, really! It was too much! If only the cottage had a phone! She could just call him, say she was fine, and tell him to stay away.

She read the note again, sensing the real desperation and anxiety with which it had been written. Most probably his conscience was troubling him, since he had abandoned her with threats of finding other company. Well, he could stew a little longer. It would do him good.

Feeling in a mood to pamper herself, she made some tea in her grandmother's silver pot and took the service on a tray into the bathroom, where she soaked her aching muscles in hot scented water. She lazed luxuriously, remembering how Gran had always brought the tea set out with pride when a special visitor came to the farm. What advice would the old lady have given her, if Lee had been able to pour out her troubles?

Forget the man: that was what her grandmother would have said. Unfortunately she couldn't do that when the note he had left kept tugging at her conscience. She would have to go to the Mill House.

She put on jeans and a thick white sweater, forsaking makeup except for a touch of mascara. After all, since she was through with Lorens, what did it matter what she looked like?

Late golden sunlight filled the woods where every branch had its share of leaves now. She disturbed a partridge that flew up with a clatter of wings and sped away toward the Mill House, which showed white beyond the trees.

Soon Lee came to the edge of the woods. In front of her, the lawn swept down to the river, past rose gardens on either side. Paving stones set in the grass led her to the white-painted footbridge, where she crossed the water to the gardens beside the house. All along the bank, weeping willows leaned as if admiring their reflections in the swift-flowing current, and the big millwheel, motionless now, had been drawn out of the water to stand behind the house.

A gravel pathway circled the building, leading to the drive at the front. Lee walked carefully, gazing up at the lovely old house and wondering if anyone were at home.

Then she heard music and saw French doors standing open to admit the late sunlight. The room inside was all shades of cream and gold, and on a curved sofa, elbows on knees, Lorens sat with his hands to his head. He appeared to be listening to the "Flying Dutchman" overture; the stirring music poured from a stereo and filled the room with a blare of horns.

Hesitantly, Lee moved up the first of two shallow steps which led to the open doors. Lorens must have seen her shadow, for his head lifted suddenly, showing her his ravaged face, and she stopped, uncertain how to play this scene.

Relief seemed to flood through him in the moment before he shot to his feet and came striding across the room, fury written in every taut line of his body.

"Where the hell have you been?" he roared at her. "I've been worried out of my mind."

"Why?" she demanded.

"Why?!" he raged. "Good God, woman—" Muttering an imprecation, he turned on his heel and went to flick a switch that silenced the music. The quietness seemed to close in on Lee as she stepped into the room.

"I'm sorry if you were worried," she said stiffly, "but I'm perfectly all right. You were being a bit melodramatic breaking into the cottage, weren't you? What did you think I'd done—slashed my wrists?"

Lorens faced her, obviously having trouble containing his temper. Beneath a chocolate-brown shirt his chest rose and fell and his hands clenched convulsively at his side. "You're a fine one to talk about melodrama," he said hoarsely. "What about that episode last night? Yes, I had visions of all sorts of horrors. The curtains were all drawn and your car was there, but though I banged on the door for ages and walked all around shouting my head off, I never got an answer. So I came back here and phoned everybody I could think of. Nobody knew where you were. What was I supposed to think? Did you deliberately leave the cottage like that just to punish me?"

"Don't be ridiculous!" Lee scoffed. "You weren't supposed to be there. How was I to know you'd go to the cottage?"

"You *should* have known!"

"Well, I didn't!"

His head lowered like a bull about to charge as he glared at her from under his lashes. "Since I found you weren't there, I've been back and forth to that damn cottage every hour or so. All day. Do you know what I've been thinking? Do you, Lee?"

She took a deep breath, calming herself. "I can imagine. I'm sorry, Lorens, but—"

"It doesn't matter," he interrupted raggedly, as he moved suddenly toward her and then wrapped her tightly in his arms. "Nothing matters except that you're safe. Oh, Lee, I was so afraid."

She let him hold her because it felt good, because it was nice to know that someone cared about her well-being enough to worry all day, even if his conscience had caused it. She let her arms slide round him as she leaned on him, her face against his shirt where she heard the quickened beat of his heart and the rush of his breathing as he sighed. A hand beneath her chin lifted her face and he bent to kiss her, ravishing her mouth while his arms threatened to crush her.

Sensing the agony in him, she was filled with a rush of gladness that caught her up in its tide and made her cling to him, her mouth making demands of its own. Quite suddenly all she wanted in the world was to have Lorens go on holding her and kissing her this way.

He pressed her head to his shoulder, his cheek resting on her hair as he muttered, "I thought you didn't want to see me again. You know it's not true, Lee. Why did you say it? What did I do?"

Unable to answer, she shook her head, her eyes closed against tears that wanted to flow.

"Come and sit down," Lorens suggested, leading her to the big curved sofa, which was covered in cream-colored leather. One of his arms curled around her, the other hand held hers. "Now, love, tell me. What was it all about? Where have you been all day? Didn't it occur to you that I'd be going quietly crazy?"

"No, it didn't," she croaked, and cleared her throat, tossing her head to get her disordered hair back into place. The dampness of tears still tangled in her lashes and she dared not look at him. Instead she kept her eyes fixed on the open neck of his brown shirt, where a pulse beat in his throat. She had a wild urge to press her lips to that pulse, to let herself melt into him and stop fighting the way she felt.

"So what happened?" he asked.

"To begin with, my car wouldn't start."

"Then why didn't you come to me for help?"

Sighing, she raised her eyes to his face and read there only concern and what appeared to be a genuine hurt that she had not turned to him. "Lorens . . . you know why. Last night—"

"Last night we were both under a strain. We both said things we didn't mean. You must have known we couldn't leave it at that."

"Yes, I suppose I did," she admitted wearily. "But all I wanted to do was get to Far Drove this morning."

"You went to the farm? But I phoned there! Sally said she had no idea—"

"You phoned her before I got there!"

"Then you *did* know I was looking for you. Why the devil didn't you phone me back?"

"I didn't know *why* you were looking for me, did I? I didn't know you were worried." She wrenched away from him and stood up. "You weren't very worried last night when you went back to the Ball! You didn't care then what happened to me. Oh . . . what's the point of arguing about it? I'm perfectly safe. I'm not suicidal. So stop feeling guilty about me and leave me alone."

Folding her arms across her chest, she turned her back on him, confused by a wave of conflicting emotions.

"I didn't go back to the Ball," he said quietly.

Startled, she glanced over her shoulder. "What?"

"I said," he repeated, getting slowly to his feet and coming toward her, "I didn't go back to the Ball. I was in no mood for socializing. I came home, and spent an hour pacing up and down trying to fathom what on earth went wrong. I almost came back to you, but in the end it seemed best to let us both sleep on it and calm down. Only I didn't get much sleep, Lee. I spent half the night wondering what the hell I'd done to make you send me away. And I still don't know."

"You didn't do anything," she sighed, staring out at the pastel sunset. The sun had dipped behind a haze of cloud and the sky was flooded with primrose, pale blue, and smudges of dove gray. Its peacefulness contrasted oddly with the storm that raged inside Lee. What was she doing here? she wondered.

109

Why did she stay and risk being drawn into the magic only Lorens could weave around her?

"Then what was it?" he said.

"Mainly—mainly it was that necklace that Sally was wearing," she told him reluctantly. "You remember you saw the things my Gran left me? That necklace should have been with them. I'd forgotten about it until I saw Sally wearing it. Oh . . ." Stepping away from him, she turned and threw out her arms helplessly. "It must sound petty and mean of me, but that's what upset me most. So I went out this morning to claim the necklace back. I was very angry about it. But Sally said she'd only borrowed it. She gave it back even before I asked for it, and then— then I offered to give it to her, but—" Her voice broke on a sob and she buried her face in her hands.

Instantly his arms were around her, drawing her to lean on him. "Don't cry, love. I don't pretend to understand, but I'm on your side. Whatever the Freemans have done, it isn't important now. I'm here. I'm with you."

Part of her knew that this was all strategy—kindness to delude her when she was at her most vulnerable. And she *was* vulnerable. Upset, lonely, needing someone.

With a sob that was half laughter at her own frailty, she flung her arms round his neck and surged up to fasten her mouth on his. He responded at once, pulling her more fully against him, his tongue touching hers, twining and probing as he edged her back to the sofa and sat down with his arms still around her.

Lee felt detached, as if she were watching from a distance, counting off the maneuvers. He laid warm kisses across her cheek, on her ear, and the tender place beneath. A part of her no longer cared whether he won or not. What did it matter if he made love to her? Part of her wanted it.

Under her hands his shirt felt smooth, and beneath it the play of muscle excited her fingertips as he shifted so that the back of the sofa no longer supported her. His lips moved from her throat to her temple, and found her mouth again. As he leaned over her she found herself slipping backwards until she was stretched along the soft leather cushions, held there by the weight of his body half across her.

"Lee!" the whisper came vibrant in her ear. "I love you, Lee."

Just at the right psychological moment, she thought with a sigh. Why did he have to lie? Couldn't he say, more truthfully, *I want you*?

As if sensing her thoughts, he raised himself on one elbow so that he could see her clearly. "What's wrong?"

"I was just thinking about Rikki," she lied. "Where is he?"

A breathless laugh shook out of him. "At a party. He won't be home yet. And the Ruffords are away for the day. There's no one here but us."

How very convenient, she thought cynically.

"Just you and me," he breathed, brushing his lips across her face as his thumb made a tentative foray beneath the waistband of her sweater.

She gasped as all her nerves came alert and Lorens smiled lazily down at her, the pupils of his eyes enlarged by desire so that the green was almost eclipsed. *You snake*, Lee thought somewhere in the depths of her mind, but by that time she was powerless in his spell.

Bending over her again, he tantalized her with soft kisses and flicks of his tongue. She could remain detached no longer. She was all woman, everything in her was crying out to him. As his hand moved slowly up across her ribs under her sweater, her arms clasped more tightly round his neck. She trembled helplessly when he cupped her breast through the fine lace of her bra, his fingers stroking, exciting her beyond sanity.

He moved to sit on the edge of the sofa, his hands beneath her raising her a little. He slipped her sweater up over her breasts and arms, pulling it over her head before dropping it on the floor.

Glancing across the swell of her barely concealed breasts, he drew her back into his arms, kissing her hungrily. She felt the warmth of him through his thin shirt as his hands ran over her back, down her spine, and up to her shoulders and her hair. He cupped her head between his hands and devoured her mouth with kisses.

Lee found her shaking fingers unfastening his shirt. She pulled the garment open and slid her hands round him, glorying in his firm strength and the feel of his flesh against hers. Her hands explored his broad back, her nerve-ends drinking in the sensations of touching his skin. Her whole body flamed with a need she had never felt so strongly before.

He stroked her back, his fingers pausing at the clasp of her bra.

"Lorens!" His name shuddered out of her. "Lorens, please—"

With horror, she heard a car coming nearer, pulling up outside. Lorens wrenched himself to his feet, buttoning his shirt, as the car door slammed and children's excited voices called.

"It's Rikki," he muttered. "Stay here. I'll delay him."

He rushed for the hall door and went out. In a daze, flushed and ashamed of herself, Lee scrambled into her sweater and, running a hand through her tousled hair, listened to Lorens speak briefly with another man at the front door. Staying where she could not be seen, she glimpsed a silver sedan with a woman in it. A man, with a boy about Rikki's age, came from the house back to the car and the whole family drove away.

Taking a few deep breaths, Lee walked slowly toward the hall, where a bright-faced Rikki, carrying a balloon and clutching a clown's mask, was telling his father about the party. Lee leaned in the doorway, her legs weak and her heart still thumping crazily.

"And we had hot dogs, and layer cake. Keith was *sick*. And we played statues, and I won. This is my prize." He dangled the mask from its cord as he caught sight of Lee, beaming at her as if delighted to see her. "Hello, Lee. See my mask?" He held it over his face and Lee shuddered.

"Ugh, it's horrible!"

Rikki showed his own frowning face. "It's supposed to be funny!"

Over his head, Lorens gave Lee a frankly sexual and regretful look, saying to his son, "Go and get your pajamas on, young man. And get washed first."

"Okay," Rikki agreed, making for the stairs where a thought occurred to him and he turned to say, glum-faced, "Have I *got* to go away tomorrow? David's going on his Dad's boat at Easter and they said I could go with them if —"

"No, I'm sorry," Lorens broke in firmly. "Your mother's expecting you. You haven't seen her since Christmas."

"Oh, hell!" Rikki mourned.

"And don't swear!"

"Why not?" the boy asked rudely. "*You* do."

As Lorens made a move toward him he turned and scrambled for saftey up the stairs. Lorens paused, a hand on the banister, and turned to Lee with a sigh.

"I'm sorry about that. We always have this trouble when he's going to Elena. But what can I do? She *is* his mother."

The question seemed rhetorical, so she made no reply. She was still trembling, her lips swollen and her flesh alive with the memory of his touch. The fire had not gone out; it was still smoldering, waiting for him to reignite the blaze.

Very slowly, Lorens advanced on her, holding her with brilliant green eyes. He lifted his hands to catch her face and she knew he was still as aroused as she was.

"He could have chosen a better moment," he said in an undertone. "Stay until he's gone to bed, will you? I'll have to let him watch TV for a while, to settle him down. He gets overexcited at these parties and then he can't sleep."

"I—I think I'd better go," Lee managed. "I'm sorry, Lorens, but . . . I ought to get back before it's dark. I really didn't mean to stay."

He watched her for a moment in silence, thoughts flickering behind his eyes. "Okay. But I'll see you soon. Not tomorrow—I've got to take Rikki to London. But Monday evening. I'll come to the cottage."

Tilting his head, he kissed her savagely, silently promising that next time they met he would finish what he had started.

Her lips still ached from the last kiss as she returned over the footbridge and through the darkening woods, her mind whirling,. What had she been going to say when Rikki's return stopped her? *Lorens, please stop?* Or, *Lorens, please make love to me?* She wasn't sure which would have come out. But of one thing she was now certain—she must not be alone with Lorens again. Being with him was much too dangerous, because every time she saw him she wanted a little bit more to believe that he was sincere.

She was herself falling into the trap she had warned Sally about, that trap of thinking that she, and she alone, might be the special woman in his life.

As she turned on the light in the cottage kitchen, she saw again the broken window with its temporary repair. And then she noticed the color that showed on the petals of the tulips, the green fading to a pale lilac-blue that astonished her.

Tulips were never that color! All shades of red, yellow and white, yes, some plain, some mottled, some verging on mauve. But never blue.

She knelt by the bucket, staring at the flowers. *Very special,* Lorens had said. *The only ones in England.* And he had not been joking. If she knew her tulips, these were the product of a new strain. Their bulbs would be worth a fortune!

Why had he brought them to her? She no longer knew what to think of his motives, but those tulips suddenly took on a new meaning and as she arranged them in several vases she touched them tenderly. They *were* special. Because Lorens had brought them.

She set the vases around the sitting room, and as she looked at the display she knew that she must not see Lorens again. If she did, she would let herself believe every word he said. He would draw her deeper into an emotional entanglement whose only result would be bitter hurt for her.

If it had remained purely physical it wouldn't have mattered; they might have enjoyed each other for a while and then parted without regret. But Lee knew she was not able to keep her emotions separate from her physical self. For her, making love and feeling love were the same.

It had to end. Now.

Seven

Despite all her rationalizing, she still hoped that Lorens might come to see her that Sunday morning before he took Rikki to London. When a car drew up outside she hurried to the door, only to droop in disappointment as she saw that her visitor was big Jim Forrester, come to fix her starter motor.

Jim began the task at once, getting himself covered with grease and oil while Lee stood by to assist when she could. Every few seconds she glanced up the lane, but each distant vehicle went rushing by on the main road. Of course Lorens wouldn't come, she told herself crossly, and it was much better that way.

She had just made mugs of coffee and brought them out when another glance up the lane made her heart leap. The blue Jaguar was sliding quietly to a halt several yards away, with Lorens driving and Rikki in the passenger seat. Trying to ignore Jim's look of open curiosity, Lee put down her coffee and walked toward the blue car as Lorens and Rikki climbed out.

"He wanted to say goodbye," Lorens said, though his glance slid beyond her to the big dark man who was watching them with interest. "And who's that?"

"That's Jim Forrester," she informed him, oddly pleased by the frown that had gathered on his brow.

"He's Gail's husband. He's very kindly come to fix my car."

"*I* could have done that for you," he said, though his frown eased a little.

"Not when you're going to London, you couldn't." She turned to the glum-faced Rikki, touching his shining hair. "Cheer up. I bet you'll enjoy yourself when you get there."

"I won't," Rikki said, and unexpectedly launched himself at her, throwing his arms around her waist. "I don't want to go, Lee!"

Disconcerted, Lee looked to Lorens for help, but he only shrugged and made a regretful face. "Don't be difficult, Rikki," he sighed. "It's only for three weeks. You mother likes to see you."

Obviously he was as reluctant as his son to have Rikki forced into yet another ritual visit to Elena. He looked so unhappy that Lee wanted to gather him in her arms, along with his son, and keep them both safe. Which was crazy.

Gently loosing the boy's grip, she bent and kissed his cheek. "You'll be home again soon. Be a good boy for Daddy."

Rikki trailed away, while his father took a slow step toward Lee, his eyes smiling and bright with messages that held her immobile.

"Do I get a kiss, too?" he asked in an undertone.

Flustered, Lee glanced at Jim, who was pretending to take no notice of the scene. Whatever she did, it would go straight back to Gail. "I don't think—"

"That's right," Lorens breathed, reaching for her. "Don't think. Just kiss me, Lee." And before she could draw breath his lips were on hers, his arms holding her warmly against him. "I'll see you tomorrow," he whispered against her mouth, kissed her again and then released her, smiling wickedly at her confusion. "'Bye, darling."

She waited until he had driven away, giving her pulse time to get back to normal before she faced Jim Forrester. Now Gail would no doubt think that Lee had fallen victim to the "local playboy," which wasn't the way of it at all. She was just stringing him along, keeping him away from Sally. Of course she was.

"This is going to be easier than I thought," Jim said. "It just needs cleaning up a bit. I'll soon have it done."

Not then, or at any other time, did he even mention Lorens.

By lunchtime, Jim had performed his oily miracle and the car started as good as new.

"I don't know how to thank you," Lee said as he cleaned his hands at the kitchen sink. "But if there's anything I can do in return—"

"There is, actually," he said with a grin. "Could you babysit with Jamie tomorrow night? I've got to go out, and Gail's got a meeting of her flower-arrangers' club. They're all getting ready for the Festival."

Tomorrow night Lorens had promised to come, she thought. She wanted to be here. But it might be wiser to be absent, even if it hurt.

"Yes, of course I'll do it," she said brightly. "I'll be glad to."

"Great. Thanks, Lee. Come and have a meal with us first. We like Jamie to know who's going to be sitting with him."

"I'd like that," she said. "Thank you. And thanks again for fixing the car."

"Oh, we men still have our uses," he laughed.

Unable to concentrate on anything, Lee decided to pay a visit to Highdyke and see Neil's mother. She had always liked Mrs. Clayton and found a warm welcome in her home, and besides she was anxious to see Neil and talk to him about Sally. Lee had more than one reason now for persuading Sally to give up her designs on Lorens.

The old house at Highdyke had been pulled down twenty years ago and a new one built nearby, separate from the farm buildings and set among lawns and trees with a duckpond by the gate. Fat ducks waddled alongside the drive, or sat preening on the lawns, as Lee drove up to the house.

Mrs. Clayton looked older than Lee remembered her, with fresh lines drawn on her face by the sorrow of her recent bereavement, but her welcome was as warm as ever, her smile as sweet. Neil, she said, had gone to a cricket club meeting but she expected him home before long.

She took Lee into her pleasant sitting room and they sat chatting as easily as if they had seen each other the previous day. For a while Mrs. Clayton talked about her husband, dwelling on happy memories before his illness, but eventually they turned to other subjects.

"I hear you were at the Tulip Ball with Lorens Van Der Haagen," Mrs. Clayton said with a smile. "I understand he's very good-looking, though I don't believe I've ever seen him—except his photo in the local paper occasionally. Your Aunt Jinnie says he's charming."

"Yes, he is," Lee admitted.

"Sally likes him, too," Mrs. Clayton observed.

"I know. And I wish she didn't. I wish she could see that Neil's much more reliable."

"But he's not as handsome and dashing as Mr. Van Der Haagen, is he? I keep telling him he'll have to pull his socks up if he wants to get anywhere with Sally. She's a live wire."

"Sally's too lively for her own good," Lee sighed. "She needs someone like Neil to steady her down. Otherwise she's going to get herself hurt, especially if she keeps hankering after Lorens. He's very plausible, Mrs. Clayton. But he only does it for his own ends."

"Does he?" Neil's mother asked gently. "There's a lot of wild gossip goes on when someone like him is concerned. He's young, wealthy, handsome—and fancy-free. He's divorced, I believe."

"Yes, he is," Lee said, wondering what point the older woman was making.

"He lives in a lovely big house," Mrs. Clayton went on. "He has all the trappings of success. It makes people jealous. So they gossip about every little thing he does. If I were you, Lee, I wouldn't believe everything you hear."

Something inside Lee clutched at this advice. Perhaps Gail had been wrong about Lorens. Lee herself had seen no sign of a parade of women in his life. The "ravishing black-haired woman" of her imagination had turned out to be Rosa Gunthorpe, who had probably gone to the Mill House in connection with the Miss Tulipland competition, and as far as Lee knew there had been no other woman at Lorens's house—not recently—except for herself!

But she *had* seen him kissing Sally by the river, and dancing with her with evident pleasure. And

121

when she told him Sally was her cousin he *had* seemed disconcerted.

Oh, Lorens. Lorens! If only she could make up her mind about him!

She was taking her leave at the front door of Highdyke when Neil drove up in a red Chevette. Grinning broadly, he came to join them and draped a friendly arm around Lee's shoulders.

"Trying to avoid me?" he asked. "Stay and have some tea. I just passed Sally up the road. She'll be here any minute."

"I'll go and put a fresh kettle on," Mrs. Clayton said. "Yes, do stay, Lee. We'll all have tea together. It will be nice."

As his mother returned to the house, Lee smiled wryly at her old friend. "I doubt if Sally will appreciate my company. Perhaps I'd better go. But Neil . . . if you want her, stop being so—" She stopped as a movement drew her eyes away. Sally had appeared on Lady Sue, riding through the gateway by the pond.

She drew rein on seeing Lee and Neill, then kicked her heels into the mare's flanks and dragged on the reins, turning Lady Sue round.

"Sally!" Neil called, starting down the drive, but before he had taken more than a few steps she was gone, at a wild gallop that took her out of sight behind a cluster of trees in a corner of the graden.

Saddened by her cousin's abrupt departure, Lee watched as Neil trudged back to join her. "I'm sorry," she sighed. "I ought not to have come. Neil, I've done my best. It's up to you now. If you don't make a move she's ging to find someone else."

"Like Lorens Van Der Haagen?" he asked with a grimace. "I don't know what to do about it, Lee. I can't force myself on her if she doesn't want me."

"Have you tried? Why don't you take her somewhere special? Buy her dinner, have some wine. Romance her."

"She wouldn't go out with me," Neil said glumly. "I'm all right as a friend—I mean, we go for walks and we talk. But I can't seem to get any further than that. Suppose I ask her out and she says no? What then?"

Lee stared at him, not believing her ears. "You've never taken her out?"

"Well, no, not really. Only to things like the Ball, when we make a foursome with her parents. I get so tongue-tied, Lee. I say all the wrong things. I'm scared even to hold her hand."

No wonder Sally had said he was slow! Lee thought in exasperation. "And you're surprised when she falls for someone like Lorens?!" she exclaimed. "He doesn't wait to make sure he's welcome, I can assure you. He finds out, in the easiest possible way—he just does it."

"Well, I suppose you'd know all about that," Neil said with a sidelong look that made her flush. "But it doesn't matter to him, does it? If one woman turns him down there's always another waiting. But for me . . . Sally's the most important thing in my life. If she turned me down, I might just as well be dead."

Lee heard the subdued anguish in his voice and saw that his eyes were moist. "Then why don't you tell her so?" she asked.

"Because she'd laugh at me. And if that happened I'd shoot myself!"

He slammed into the house and after a moment Lee got into her car, shaken by the emotions that had roared through the usually calm young farmer.

Poor Neil. Sally was a fool not to see how he felt about her, but if Neil dared not even touch her hand how was the girl supposed to know he loved her? Someone ought to tell her.

Reaching the gate, she turned in the direction of Far Drove with every intention of finding Sally and . . . Her foot stabbed the brake, bringing her up short. Idiot! She had already interfered too much, and what good had it done? Sally still had her sights fixed on Lorens. If Lee told her what Neil had said, she would probably laugh, just as he feared.

She turned in the opposite direction, vowing to keep out of her cousin's affairs from now on.

She turned her mind to work, bent over the dining table in the main room of the cottage, with notes spread around her as she worked in the framework of her book. She had decided to base it on a month-by-month account, beginning in June when the parade committee met to decide on a theme for the following year.

"Then it's my job to go around and persuade people to act as sponsors," Peter Atkinson had said. "Companies like banks, or local firms such as Haagen Bulbs, even British Rail, will pay for a float. Actually, British Rail puts on about twenty-five special trains to bring people in to see the parade every year. And every inch of spare space is used for cars and buses."

He had shown her aerial photographs of the town, with blocks taken up by buses and cars, and people massing all around the route of the parade.

"We raise a lot of funds for charity," he had added, "but some people come along and watch the floats without spending any money, If only I could put up road blocks and charge a toll fee, we could make a fortune. It's the greatest free show in Britain."

In among details of how the parade came about every year, Lee planned to weave the history of tulips, which first came from Turkey to Holland four hundred years ago. In the seventeenth century, she had discovered, the Netherlands experienced a tulip-mania during which a single bulb might change hands for as much as a thousand pounds; by contrast, during the cruel winter of 1945, starving Dutch people had been driven to eat flower bulbs merely to stay alive.

In the back of her mind, she kept thinking about Lorens. Did it bother him to see his wife? Was it his philandering that had driven Elena away? Or could Mrs. Clayton be right and the gossip about him largely exaggerated?

Remembering the things he had said and the way he had behaved, Lee was more and more inclined to believe that he had been sincere. She had been wrong to judge him on the basis of gossip. So what if she had seen him kissing Sally?

Unfortunately, somewhere inside her there remained a niggling doubt. Her feelings for him had grown to such an extent that she might be blinding herself to the truth about him.

Knowing Lorens would be at his office, she spent the following day engaged in more research. She went to meet Kees Van Driel, the designer of the floats, and spent some time chatting with Peter Atkinson's secretary at Springfields Gardens; then she called again at the cool warehouse where Geoff Dodds the blacksmith and Pete Bell the strawman were still busy making the floats. This time Pete was fastening straw around the figure of a cartoon giant stepping down from a bean-stalk, while Geoff worked on metal bands, forming wine jars for Ali Baba's thieves.

All through the day, Lee was aware that Lorens had promised to visit her that evening, and that she would not be there because she had agreed to babysit with Jamie Forrester. She almost phoned him to explain, but those niggling doubts remained. If he came to the cottage he would want to make love to her; it was safer to stay clear and avoid being alone with him if possible. His presence always managed to scramble her common sense.

By late afternoon she arrived at Gail's bungalow and found her friend hurriedly preparing an evening meal.

"Goodness, I'm glad to see you," Gail gasped. "Would you mind laying the table for me? I had to go into town today to collect some curtains from the cleaners and then I went to Mum's for lunch and got talking. I was out for hours. The tablecloth's in the sideboard drawer."

The dining alcove led off the kitchen, so the two were able to talk as Lee arranged cutlery and Gail dealt with simmering saucepans. Lee chatted about her day's research, trying to avoid the subject of Lorens. But as she went into the kitchen to get salt and pepper for the table, Gail said:

"Have you seen Lorens Van Der Haagen lately?"

"Not since yesterday," Lee said, ready for arguments about the kiss Jim had witnessed.

Rubbing her hands on her apron, Gail leaned on the worktop, her face so full of despair that Lee's heart contracted.

"It's no good, I've got to tell you," Gail blurted. "I saw him today. You know that boutique where Sally works is opposite the cleaners? Well, I was waiting for them to find my curtains when I saw Lorens Van Der Haagen walk up and stand outside the boutique, as though he were waiting for someone. Then Sally came out to join him and they went off together. I couldn't help myself, Lee—I watched where they were heading. They went into that expensive restaurant just down the street. He was taking her to lunch."

Lee's first reaction was disbelief. Lorens wouldn't take Sally on a lunch date!

But why should Gail lie? From her expression it was all too obvious that she hated to inform Lee of what she had seen. It was Lorens who had lied, and Lee had almost fooled herself into believing him.

"Lee, I'm sorry," Gail whispered. "It does matter to you, doesn't it?"

"No," Lee denied, her voice hoarse with self-disgust. She shook herself, her lips curved in a bitter smile. "No, it's only confirmed what I knew all along. Don't worry about it, Gail. I'm glad you told me. You've probably saved me from making the biggest mistake of my life."

But the pain inside her said that the rescue had come a little late.

Jamie slept peacefully all evening while Lee watched television and tried to shut her mind to thoughts of Lorens. She was glad now—fiercely glad—that she had had a good reason not to be at the cottage, for she had no doubt that Lorens would keep their date, even after lunching with Sally. He had probably been seeing Sally all this time, keeping both of them dangling.

127

April showers which had drizzled all day turned to a heavy downpour as, eventually, she drove home late that night. Since she had been out all day she had not lit the fire, and the cottage felt cold as the wind lashed rain across the windows. Shivering, Lee made herself a hot drink and went to bed, where she lay thinking bleak thoughts about men who preyed on the weakness of women.

She was still wide awake, alternately berating herself for her stupidity and aching inside for want of a man she knew to be worthless, when an urgent hammering on the door downstairs brought her upright in the bed. For a moment she listened, wondering what emergency prompted someone to her door at that hour.

Rain pattered across her window, blown by the wind that sighed gustily in the woods. The knocking came again, a heavy and determined pounding that made her slip out of bed and pull on her robe. She tied the belt as she ran down the stairs blinking against the sudden light.

When she opened the door the wind rushed in, bringing a burst of rain that made her shiver as she stared in disbelief at the sight of Lorens on her doorstep, grim-faced and with his hair plastered wetly to his head. His sweater was wet, too, and the bottoms of his trousers splashed.

"Where the devil have you been all evening?" he demanded, pushing past her without ceremony.

Lee closed the door on the elements, her thoughts in disarray. "I've been out. Lorens . . . you surely didn't come through the woods in the dark, in this weather?"

"I left my car down the lane a way," he replied, giving her a furious look. "I didn't want to alarm you in case you had company."

"Company?" Lee said blankly.

"Yes, company! Is there someone here? Perhaps I'll look for myself."

As he charged up the stairs, a bewildered Lee said, "I don't know what you're talking about. I've been out babysitting."

Lorens stopped, looking down at her across the banister. "Babysitting? Where?"

"In Spalding. For my friend Gail." She was beginning to recover from her astonishment enough to be angry at his gall in bursting in and making accusations.

"Did you forget we had a date tonight?" he demanded.

Lee clutched the neck of her wrap a little tighter, huddled into herself. "No, I didn't forget. I just decided I didn't want to see you."

"Really?" The word drawled out of him, thick with scorn. "Does it amuse you to have me running around after you? Make you feel good?"

"I wasn't even sure you'd come!" Lee cried. "You might have been out with one of your other women. Sally, for instance. I gather you had lunch with her today."

A frown brought his brows down over eyes that gleamed coldly beneath a tangle of wet hair. "Are you spying on me now? Who told you that?"

"Someone I trust. Someone who wouldn't lie to me."

Very slowly, he began to come back down the stairs, his face and voice devoid of emotion. "I see. So now you think you own me, do you? Well, I've got news for you, Miss Summerfield. No woman has me in her pocket. No woman ever will, not again. One fiasco was enough for me."

As he reached the bottom of the stairs, Lee backed away, edging into the darkened sitting room as he advanced on her. With his wet hair, glittering eyes, and grim face he was a terrifying sight, exuding powerful menace.

"You said you loved me!" she gasped.

Harsh laughter, with no amusement in it, caught her like a blow to her heart. "Wasn't that what you wanted to hear?" he said scornfully. "Wasn't that what you'd been angling for?"

"Lorens!" she cried, shaking with nerves. "Please stop this. You're wet through. Go home and get dry. Please!"

"You're right," he said. "I am wet. But I'll deal with that."

Fastening his hands in the waist of his sweater, he removed it in one smooth rippling movement, also taking off the T-shirt he was wearing beneath. His eyes glittered beneath tousled hair and Lee's head swam with panic as she stared in disbelief at his muscular torso. What on earth was he planning to do?

She backed away further, her eyes huge and dark with fear in her pale face. The shadows of the sitting room closed around her. As Lorens stepped into the shaft of light through the doorway she gasped, for the back of the couch prevented her from moving farther.

"Please don't do this, Lorens," she begged. "Please—"

Before she could move, he strode toward her. His hands shot out and fastened on her shoulders, his fingers bit through her thin wrap. He pulled her toward him so sharply that her head tipped back and she was left staring fearfully up at him, her hands flat on his naked chest in an effort to keep him away.

She smelled whiskey on his breath, though he wasn't drunk. He was quite coldly, deadly sober.

"You're not afraid of me, are you?" he asked in a low voice. "I won't hurt you, Lee. That isn't my style."

His glance slid to her mouth, making her tremble even more violently. Like a rabbit hypnotized by a snake, she hung helpless in his grasp as he slowly, slowly, lowered his head until nearness drove his face out of focus and she closed her eyes, her arms braced against him in vain resistance.

She clamped her teeth, keeping her lips pressed tightly together to prevent his invasion as he kissed her, and after a moment he lifted his head.

"What's wrong with you?" he asked in a low, taunting voice. "You weren't so particular last Saturday."

"Last Saturday I thought you cared about me!" she got out, turning her head away.

He gave another unpleasant laugh. "Then we were both deluded, weren't we? Come on, Lee, we're both adults. Why fight me? You know I want you. And you want me, too."

One arm clamped round her waist while the other hand fastened on her jaw, bringing her back to face him. Soft kisses tantalized her lips, mingled with sensual flicks of his tongue. Despite herself, her jaw muscles relaxed and gave him access to the sweetness of her mouth. She felt her resistance melting as her body began to respond to the wild urging of his kisses.

As his hand relaxed, moving down to caress her throat, she made a desperate effort to escape, wrenching her head sideways and back. "No! Lorens—"

He moved closer, his body pinning her against the couch. Bending his head, he brushed his lips down the arched curve of her throat, causing tremors deep inside her. His arm still encircled her waist, holding her molded to him, but his free hand caressed her neck, slipping beneath her wrap to her shoulder. His mouth explored each new inch of exposed flesh. He slowly pushed the wrap aside, along with the thin strap of her nightgown, until the garments slid down her arm.

Lee found her own hands spread against his flesh, feeling the heat that rose from him. No longer were her hands a barrier, but a communication, her fingers enjoying the touch of firm muscle rippling beneath skin that grew warmer with every minute. In her head she knew this was all wrong, but he worked magic on her senses, bringing every part of her alive.

A last vestige of sanity made her say brokenly, "You'll catch your death."

"Then warm me," he replied hoarsely, lifting his mouth to hers. That kiss took full possession of her. Shuddering, she let her arms slide round him as her lips parted beneath his onslaught and fire burned inside her, fanned by the sensuous movement of his body against hers as he held her with his hips. She felt the belt of her robe slide undone and then he was pulling the wrap open, touching her body through the thin silk of her nightgown.

Tremors shook her as he leaned farther over her, bending her backwards, his lips tracing a tingling pathway down her throat as his hands bared both her shoulders and then her breasts. Cool air caressed her skin, but Lorens warmed her with the heat of his hands and his mouth as he stroked and kissed, sweetly tormenting her breasts while he eased the wrap from her arms.

He straightened, clasping her to him as he looked down into her face with burning eyes. Against her bare breasts his chest rose and fell, his breath coming swiftly, rasping in the quiet room. She trembled, feeling his burning need of her, but not even the half-light could disguise the taut lines of anger that mingled with desire in his face.

"Why are you shaking?" he demanded hoarsely. "Are you cold? Let's go upstairs."

She quivered uncontrollably, as if afflicted with ague, and could not reply. She hung helpless in his arms, vividly aware of his naked flesh melting with hers. Only the pressure of his body kept her nightgown from sliding from her hips, so that if he moved away just a fraction she would be totally nude. Her body longed for a consummation, but her mind cried treachery.

"Well?" he growled.

"I've never—never—" The words wouldn't come, but she felt the surprise that ran through him.

He swore, with a vicious disgust that made her wince. He bent suddenly and swept her off her feet, up into his arms where he held her cruelly tight for a moment before he leaned forward and dropped her onto the couch, where she sprawled in a daze.

"Thank your lucky stars I've got some self-control," he grated, his voice harsh across her nerves. "Next time you lead a man on, you might not be so lucky. Goodbye. Lee."

He swung away, another expletive jerking out of him as he caught the edge of the table. Lee heard one of the vases of tulips topple with a crack and a soft spash of water; then Lorens was gone. She heard small sounds from the hall as he replaced his sweater, then the front door slammed shut.

Dazed and shivering, Lee sat up and stared at the scattered tulips lying spilled in a pool of water on the velour cloth.

She had had a narrow escape, but somewhere inside her the dreamer wept for what might have been. Gail had been right all along—Lorens's charm and tenderness had been a fake. But even now Lee couldn't convince herself of it entirely. He had played the part too well.

Until tonight. There had been no tenderness in him tonight.

Eight

For a while, as she filled her days with work on her book, she expected to see Lorens at any time. Every evening she spent at the cottage her ears were tuned for the sound of his car, or a knock at the door, and she wasn't sure whether she hoped for it or dreaded it.

She stayed away from home as much as possible, spending evenings with Gail or going alone to the cinema, or simply driving around until darkness fell.

Gradually the blue tulips opened wide and began to die, mute barometers of her relationship with Lorens. She had believed they meant something special, but obviously that had been another delusion. But it still hurt when, as she sat working one evening, the first petal dropped with a soft plop onto a notebook lying open on the table. Lee picked it up, feeling its still-silky texture. Blue tulips—she hadn't had a chance to ask him about them.

Leaning her heavy head in her hands, she thought about his last visit to the cottage, able now to see it with detachment. How angry he had been! How different from the man she had known before. His sole purpose had been to make her submit to him, and he had almost accomplished it. Almost—

yet what had stopped him? Her protestations of sexual innocence?

Why had he been so angry? What had made him think she might be with another man? Lee began to see puzzles she could not answer. What had happened between their brief meeting on Sunday morning, when he had brought Rikki to say goodbye, and his stormy arrival in the rain late at night? Surely he hadn't imagined she might be involved with Jim Forrester? No, that was ludicrous.

He had been genuinely angry—an anger born of jealousy and suspicion. Why? What had he thought, seen, heard?

Among the bitter memories of the things he had said and done that night, one illogical sentence now clamored for explanation. *We were both deluded, weren't we?* he had said. Was it possible that he had thought she cared for him, and that it mattered to him whether she cared? Or was she clutching at straws, trying to find excuses for him again, because she couldn't bear to think he had cheated her? Because she missed him?

In the silence the fire spat softly, while ouside the wind sighed through the new leaves in the woods. Lee at last faced up to the truth of the aching misery she had been trying to ignore for more than two weeks. What she was experienceing was loneliness— loneliness that only one man could ease. And since that one man was unattainable she would have to live with her loneliness, and with the unshakable feeling that if only she had behaved differently she might have won him for herself.

Unable to stay at the cottage, which was haunted with memories, she took a day off from her project and drove far from Spalding. The countryside was at its best, all the trees wore shimmering green leaves, abundant flowers and blossoms spread their glory of pink and white. In the marshland now, rows of color painted the fields, strips of yellow and all shades of red turning, as one approached, into a million swaying tulips.

But as far as she drove she could not escape from that numb ache and the unanswered questions that plagued her. She wanted to know the truth, however hurtful it might be. Being left with doubts was much worse than knowing for sure that she had been taken for a fool.

She came back to the cottage determined to get on with her work and forget her troubles. But as she opened the front door she was alarmed by a loud clatter and bang from the kitchen, accompanied by a high-voiced cry. Heart in mouth, she ran down the hall and flung open the kitchen door, prepared for anything—anything but what actually met her eyes.

It was Rikki, sprawled on the floor beside an overturned stool, with cupboard doors open above him.

Her feet crunched spilled sugar as she bent anxiously over him. "Rikki, whatever happened? Are you hurt? What are you . . ." The words died as she saw what he clutched in his hand—her Georgian silver sugar bowl, from which sugar had spread halfway across the floor.

Wailing, Rikki turned over, hiding his face as loud sobs shook through him.

Swiftly, Lee glanced about the room, guessing what had happened. She had kept meaning to get someone to put a new pane in the window, but had put it off. Now the cardboard that Lorens had sealed around the gap was lying on the drainer, and the window was open. So Rikki had broken in, presumably to steal the silver.

But what was he doing here? He was supposed to be in London, at least until the following weekend.

"Rikki . . ." She laid a hand on the thin, shaking shoulder. "Are you hurt? Please talk to me. I'm not going to be angry." Leaning over him, she lifted him and peered at his scarlet, tear-stained face. "Don't cry, Rikki. It's all right."

The sugar bowl rolled across the floor as he let it go and threw his arms round her neck, weeping against her. "I didn't mean it, Lee. I didn't mean it. I'm sorry."

"Shush, darling," she comforted, kneeling on the floor with his weight across her thighs. She held him close, smoothing the silky fair hair and cursing his unknown mother. Something traumatic must have happened to make Rikki behave in this way. He was crying bitterly, hopelessly, a little lost soul needing comfort.

"Don't tell Dad!" he begged between sobs. "Oh, please don't tell Dad. I didn't know what to do, Lee. I wanted to run away."

Gathering that he was more frightened and unhappy than injured, Lee calmed him down, sat him at the table and gave him a glass of milk. She sat close beside him, stroking the hair from his forehead. His face and hands were filthy, his clothes smudged and crumpled.

"Now tell me about it," she suggested softly.

Rikki gave her a tearful look from under long fair lashes, reminding her sharply of his father. "I ran away. And I'm not going back! Don't make me go back!"

"Hush!" She gathered him into her arms, sitting him on her knee even though he was a little big for such babying. "Why did you run away, Rikki?"

"Because . . ." More tears burst out of him and he buried his face in the curve of her neck, thin arms nearly choking her as he sobbed something that sounded like, "I don't want to go to Switzerland."

"Who said anything about going to Switzerland?" Lee asked, perplexed.

"Mummy did! Mummy and Uncle Heini. I heard them talking. They said they'd take me away from Dad. They said I could live with them in Switzerland. So I ran away."

Lee held him away from her, looking down at him. "You ran away from *London*? But how did you manage to get here?"

"On the train. I had enough money for a ticket, so I went to the station and got on a train. A lady told me which one I wanted. And then I walked all the way from Spalding. Only I didn't dare go home. Dad'll be furious. Oh, don't tell him, Lee! Let me stay with you."

"But he'll be worried sick!" Lee exclaimed. "When did you leave your mother's house? This morning?"

"Yes. Before breakfast. I had a hot dog later on, when I was trying to find the station. And when I got off the train I didn't have any money left, so—so I came here. I saw how Dad got in that time. It was easy. I was going to —" Doubt clouded his small face and he couldn't look at her. "I thought I could sell that sugar bowl. You did say it was worth a lot of money. But I'd have paid you back, honest I would. Honest!"

"Yes, well, we'll talk about that later," Lee said, sighing. "It was very wrong of you. You know that.

139

But if you promise me never to do such a thing again, I won't tell your Dad about it. But he'll have to know the rest."

"But he'll send me back!" he wailed. "I don't want to go to Switzerland. I don't like Uncle Heini. I want to stay with my Dad."

She held him closely, resting her cheek on his soft hair and knowing exactly how he felt. "Of course you do, Rikki. And your Dad wants you, too. He won't let you go away. But, don't you see? they'll have told him you vanished. He'll be worried about you. We must go and tell him you're safe."

Rikki didn't want to go; he was terrified of Lorens's anger. Remembering how furious Lorens had been when she herself had been missing, Lee sympathized with his son, but eventually she persuaded him to get into her car, though only after she had promised to speak to Lorens before Rikki had to face him.

Pushing her own feelings to the back of her mind, thinking only of the child's best interests, she drove to the Mill House and parked on the gravel drive. Rikki slid down in the seat, cowering there with a look of woe, as if trying to hide.

"Stay there," Lee instructed. "I'll see your Dad first. And you know—if he's angry, it's only because he's been worried."

Lorens must be at home; his Jaguar stood in a corner of the drive by a bed of pink and blue hyacinths. Straightening herself, Lee crunched across the gravel to the main door and rang the bell.

After a moment, she heard Lorens say faintly, "All right, Mrs. Rufford, I'll get it."

The door opened and he stood there elegant in light-colored slacks and his dark brown shirt. Not

140

even his surpirse at seeing her could disguise the harassed lines on his face.

"Well?" he barked, glowering.

"I've got Rikki in my car," she said. "He's all right. Lorens—"

As he tried to get past she threw herself in front of him, one hand on his arm, the other flat against his shirtfront. The contact sent electric sparks along her nerves, but it stopped him and as he glared down at her Lee's heart twisted. *I love you, Lorens,* she thought hopelessly.

"He's in a terrible state," she said, pleading for his understanding. "He came to me because he was afraid to come home. Please don't be angry with him. He needs —"

He glanced down at her hands and back at her face with such withering contempt that she snatched her hands away, clenching them tightly. Then he pushed roughly past her and went to her car, opening the passenger door to reveal his wan-faced son.

"Rikki!" The hoarse whisper came back to Lee as he took his son from the car and lifted him in his arms, where the boy straddled his waist and fastened small arms tight about his father's neck. For a moment Lorens stood quite still, just holding his son in relief at having found him, then he walked back to the house, his eyes moist as they met Lee's over the child's shoulder.

"You'd better come in," he said.

"No, I won't—"

"I said," he repeated through his teeth, his eyes glinting, "come in. I want to know what happened."

Tense as a bowstring before the arrow flies, Lee followed the pair into the gold and cream sitting

141

room. Through the French doors she could see the willows bending along the riverbank, and the memory of what had happened here only a few weeks ago made her pause, tears flooding her head as she watched Lorens with his son.

She loved them both, the man and the boy, with a hurting, despairing love that wrenched at her heart.

Lorens was not angry. He set his son in one of the pale leather chairs and knelt beside him, firmly but gently drawing the story out of the unhappy child. Rikki didn't say much more than he had told Lee. He had heard his mother and his "uncle" talking about taking him to Switzerland, away from Lorens. So he had run away, only to be so afraid of what his father migh say that he dared not go home to the Mill House but had gone instead to the cottage.

"I got in through the window—like *you* did," he said.

For the first time, Lorens turned to glance at Lee with a fierce expression that blamed her for making him worried enough to break into her cottage with his son as a witness.

"I was going to steal her sugar bowl and sell it," Rikki added in a mutter that made his father swing around to face him again.

"You *what*?" Lorens said softly.

"I didn't mean it!" Rikki cried, jumping from his chair to run and throw himself at Lee. "I had to tell him the truth, Lee. Will the police take me away?"

"No, of course they won't," she soothed, hugging him.

Very slowly, as if all his muscles were stiff, Lorens got to his feet. "I think you'd better go and wash, Rikki. We'll talk about this later. And don't worry—

I'll speak to your mother. She won't be taking you away. That much I can promise you."

"I never want to stay with her again," Rikki said, clutching Lee's hand as if she were his lifeline. "Can Lee come with me?"

Lorens shot her a lightning look that faded as he sighed. "Yes, if that's what you want. Just go and get clean. I'll ask Mrs. Rufford to get some food ready. I assume you're hungry?"

"Starving," Rikki said. "Come on, Lee."

Torn between the boy's obvious need of her and his father's no less obvious reluctance to have her stay, Lee hesitated when Rikki pulled at her hand. "I didn't intend to stay. I wouldn't be here at all if I'd been able to phone and—"

"Oh, go with him," Lorens said, brushing off her explanations with a weary hand. Suddenly he looked tired and wretched. "I'd better phone Elena."

"Come on," Rikki urged again, dragging Lee with him into the hall and up the stairs.

The same gold carpet lay everywhere, along the upper hall and even into bedrooms which she glimpsed through partly open doors. Rikki's room lay at a front corner of the house. Evening sunlight streamed through the window onto a cream candlewick bedspread and walls decorated with color posters of birds. On a chest, stuffed animals sat waiting for their owner to play, while a big toy box stood in a corner.

Rikki opened his toy box, taking out things to show her.

"Your Dad said you were to wash," Lee reminded him, feeling awkward about being there.

"I don't like getting washed. I like to have a bath." He pulled a boat from under a pile of other toys, and leapt to his feet. "Let's go and play dive-bombing. You run the bath for me. Plenty of bubbles." He frowned at her as she lifted a questioning eyebrow. "I mean—*please* will you run the bath? The taps are too stiff for me."

The taps were, indeed, turned off so hard that even Lee had trouble moving them, but soon water thundered in, raising bubbles and sending up steam to cloud the mirror tiles. A naked Rikki ran in, arms full of floatable toys, which he piled with him into the bath. Lee sat on the carpet watching him, wondering at his resilience. Now that he was safely at home, all his troubles of an hour before seemed to have been forgotten.

For herself, she was only too aware that this peace could not last. Sorrow sat heavily on her and her mind remained with the weary man downstairs, who now had the task of sorting out the problems Rikki had created.

However, Rikki's innocent pleasure in his games soon drew her to play with him, dropping a wet sponge to sink the boats, ducks, and plastic bottles. But her thoughts were on Lorens.

She jumped when Lorens said furiously from behind her, "What's going on here? I just said to *wash*. Can't you do anything you're told?"

While Lee got to her feet and moved into a corner, he pulled out the plug, grabbed a towel and bent to swing his squirming son out of the bath as easily as if he had been a baby. "Shut up!" he snapped when Rikki complained. He dried the child swiftly and none too gently, making Lee wonder if she ought to leave. From the stormy look on Lorens's face, his phone call to Elena had not been a friendly one.

"Now go and get dressed," he said after a while, giving Rikki a push toward the door. "Mrs. Rufford's got some supper for you."

The towel-clad Rikki plodded out, subdued by his father's mood. Sighing, Lorens straightened and glowered at Lee beneath disheveled fair hair, standing between her and the door.

"No wonder he turns to you," he said bitterly. "You let him do exactly as he likes. Oh . . . don't bother making excuses. I can see for myself what's happening."

"I didn't plan this, you know," Lee said in a low voice. "What was I supposed to do—write you a letter? I knew you'd be worried. That's the only reason I came."

He fixed her with an unpleasant look. "How very neighborly of you, Miss Summerfield."

Beside her, the bath water gurgled and she glanced down to see remnants of suds draining round the scattered toys. When she looked back at Lorens she found him regarding her with clouded eyes.

"Why the hell did you have to come here?" he muttered.

"I didn't have much choice! Should I have sent Rikki home alone?"

"That isn't what I meant!"

"Then what did you mean?"

"Nothing. Forget it." He swung around as Rikki scampered past the door on his way to the kitchen. Another heavy sigh escaped Lorens and he moved out into the hall, watching his son disappear. "I phoned Elena," he said.

Lee moved to the doorway, worriedly watching his profile. "What did she say?"

145

"She's getting married again to this . . . Heini, or whatever his name is. He's Swiss. They'll be living in Geneva. So now, rather late in the game, she fancies she might like to be a full-time mother. She asked me to let her have Rikki permanently."

"And what did you tell her?"

He flashed her a furious look that had pain behind it. "I wouldn't like to repeat what I said. The divorce court gave *me* custody and I'm keeping him. Rikki's *my* son. He's the only worthwhile thing to come out of that so-called marriage. Elena may think she's found the right man at last, but she's never happy with one man for long. I give it two years at the most. Do you think I'd risk having Rikki's life turned upside down again?"

"I'm sure you wouldn't," Lee said, hurting for him, "especially when you know he doesn't want to go with her. He doesn't even like visiting her."

Lorens turned on her angrily. "I know that! Don't tell me about my own son. He's not your concern. Stay away from him, Lee."

"I didn't—" she began, but the tears she had kept bottled inside suddenly broke loose and blinded her. She darted along the hall, trying to escape, but by a half-open door his hand came unyieldingly around her arm, swinging her back to face him.

"Tears now, right?" he said quietly. "Every trick in the book. Don't you ever give up, Lee?"

She gaped at him, her eyes scalding. "Tricks? *You* accuse *me* of . . . Oh, let me go!"

Hard hands on her upper arms forced her backwards, despite her struggles, into the nearby room, where he closed the door with his foot. One sidelong glance told Lee they were in his bedroom. His sweater was lying across a chair and male toiletries were on a low dressing table. She also saw the expanse of a double bed covered with a gold silk counterpane, which made memories of their last encounter at the cottage rise up and threaten to suffocate her.

Wide-eyed and trembling, she stared up at his taut face. "So all right!" she croaked. "Go ahead, if it will make you feel better. You're bigger than me. You're stronger. Go ahead and—"

"Shut up!" he snapped in exactly the same tone he had used to Rikki. Then he jerked her toward him and fastened his mouth on hers, punishing her with a fierce kiss that both repelled and excited her.

After a moment, he pushed her roughly away. Staggering, she fell backwards across the bed, a hand to her bruised lips as she stared in terror at the glowering man who stood over her like a demon. His glance swept over her as though he were remembering the way she looked naked, and Lee caught her breath.

"Just what do you take me for?" he asked in disgust. "Oh, come on, Lee, stop the play-acting. I know what you're up to. Sally told me all about it."

"Sally?" she managed, uncomprehending.

"Yes, Sally! I suppose you thought you were being very subtle, but it's surprising how a jealous woman can see through her rival's ploys. You're not fooling her for a minute—or me. Get up off that bed, for God's sake!" He turned away, hand raking through his hair as he went to stare out of the window at the willows and the river, with the woods beyond.

Feeling chilled, Lee pushed herself to a sitting position. So Sally had guessed her plan—guessed that Lee was encouraging Lorens on purpose. And she had told him so. They must be more closely involved than Lee had dreamed. Was Sally really so infatuated with him that she didn't care what he did, as long as she had a share in him?

"I notice you're not bothering to deny it," Lorens said in a low voice. "At least I'm grateful for that. Just go away, Lee. Get out of my house. Get out of my life."

"For *her* sake?" Lee asked hoarsely.

Frowning, Lorens swung around. "What?"

But before she could reply, Mrs. Rufford's voice called urgently along the hall outside, "Mr. Lorens! Oh, Mr. Lorens!"

Cursing under his breath, he strode across and threw the door open. "What now?"

Mrs. Rufford appeared, looked disapprovingly past him at Lee, and said, "Oh, there you are. There's a phone call for you."

"For me?" Lee said, a hand to her buzzing head as she struggled off the bed. "But no one knows I'm here. Who is it?"

"It's a Mr. Clayton. Neil Clayton, he said. He didn't say what it was about, but it sounded urgent."

Lorens stepped aside to let her pass, giving her a bleak look that made her want to weep. Maybe she had started out with some crazy idea about saving Sally from his clutches, but *she* was the one who had got trapped—trapped into loving a man who had no heart. And now he hated her, though she still didn't understand why.

Following Mrs. Rufford's ample figure, she found herself in a downstairs room whose lower walls were lined with bookcases. Modern paintings hung on the walls above, mostly stylized representations of tulip fields and local landscapes. A desk stood across one corner, and the phone was on a low table

148

near the windowseat, which was made of plump brown leather. Here again, the gold carpet stretched beneath her feet, though the yellow tones that decorated the rest of the house were relieved by darker masculine colors.

"You can use that extension," Mrs. Rufford said with a nod at the phone. "I'll put the kitchen one down when I get back there."

"Thank you." Still puzzled as to how Neil had known to call her at the Mill House, Lee picked up the phone. "Hello? Neil?"

"Lee?" He sounded troubled. "I'm sorry to bother you, but I'm afraid I've got bad news—not too bad, but . . . There's been an accident. Sally and your aunt are in the hospital."

Stunned, Lee sank down on the windowseat, her glance flicking to Lorens, who had appeared in the doorway. "*Both* of them?" she breathed. "Why, what happened?"

"Somebody was giving them a lift back from town. The car went into a ditch. I think they'll be all right, but they've both got to stay in the hospital at least for a few days. Sally's got a concussion and they think your aunt's broken a couple of ribs. I haven't got any more details at the moment. But your uncle's going to need someone here—for moral support, if nothing else. I thought you might want to come."

"Yes, of course I will. I'll be there as soon as I can. Thanks for letting me know, Neil. I'll see you soon. 'Bye."

She hardly noticed the faintly sardonic smile on Lorens's face as he said, "Well?"

"It's my aunt—and Sally. There was an accident. They're both in the hospital."

"I'm sorry to hear that," he said gravely.

"Don't you care?" Lee cried.

"Of course I care. But what do you expect me to do about it? I've enough problems of my own at the moment. No doubt you'll deal with it with your customary efficiency."

"Oh, you're—you're unbelievable!" Lee exclaimed in disgust. "You just don't give a damn about anybody but yourself, do you? You sail through life just using people. I only hope this proves to Sally what a rotten beast you really are."

She tried to get past him, but again he caught her arm, his fingers biting into her flesh. "Say that again."

Flinging her head up, she glared at him with sparking brown eyes. "You heard what I said. Will you *please* take your hands off me?"

"Not until you explain," he said grimly, both hands fastened on her shoulders, and shaking her a little. "That's the second time you've implied I've got some special interest in Sally. Just because I took her to lunch—"

"That isn't all you've done and you know it!" she flung at him. "Maybe you don't realize how she feels about you, but *I* do—she's warned me off enough times."

A frown drew his brows together as he searched her face, his fingers absently massaging her shoulders. "I don't understand a word you're saying, Lee."

As she opened her mouth to reply, she caught her breath at the sight of Rikki standing in the hall behind Lorens, his eyes wide with anxiety, on the edge of tears. He must have heard them quarreling, she thought with a pang of guilt and sympathy for the child.

As Lorens followed her gaze, his hands fell away from her and she moved beyond him. "I must go. I'm needed at Far Drove. 'Bye, Rikki."

The boy just looked at her, mutely miserable, and impulsively she went to him, hugging him and pressing a kiss to his hair.

"Don't look like that. You're safe at home now. Everything's all right, Rikki."

He still made no reply, only stared dumbly at his father, and when Lee glanced back she saw Lorens watching her, frowning as if her behavior puzzled him. Straightening, she said, "Be good," to the boy, and left the house.

Nine

She arrived at Far Drove to find Neil Clayton there alone. Her uncle had stayed at the hospital to await results of x-rays and tests.

"Fortunately I was here when the police came," Neil said. "Mr. Freeman left right away, and then I thought about you. I was going to ask Van Der Haagen to take you a message. I never thought you'd be here at the Mill House."

"I wouldn't have been, under normal circumstances," Lee said. "Oh, it's a long story, Neil. Thanks for calling me. You go home. Your mother will be worrying. We'll let you know when there's any news."

"Fine," he said. "I'll do that. You'll be all right here alone?"

Underneath his composure, she saw that he was worried sick. "You know, Sally's young and healthy," she reminded him. "She'll come through this."

"I hope so," he said. "'Bye, Lee."

A casserole simmered in the oven, presumably left there by Aunt Jinnie before she went into town. Lee turned the heat down a little, thinking that her uncle might be glad of a hot meal when he came in.

Eventually, after dark, lights swept into the yard and Lee went out to meet her uncle.

"It's not as bad as it might have been," he replied to her inquiry. "Your Aunt Jinnie's cracked a rib and bruised a lung, and Sally's got a lump on her head the size of an ostrich egg. She was out cold for two hours, but she came to before I left. The doctor said they'll both be all right in a few days."

"I'm glad," she said fervently, following him into the kitchen. "Shall we phone Neil and tell him?"

"No, I did that from the hospital. That's when he told me you were here. Lee, I'm grateful."

"What are families for?" she replied. "Are you ready for a meal? I thought we might have supper together. And . . . I've brought a few clothes, so if you'd like me to stay . . ."

He looked surprised, but pleased. "I wish you would. I'll be living on bread and water if I have to do for myself. And Lord knows what your Aunt Jinnie would have to say about the mess I'd make of her kitchen."

So Lee stayed, glad to be able to help. And without her aunt's sharp tongue and Sally's jealousy to spoil things, she was almost happy playing housewife at Far Drove with old Jed around the place and Uncle Bert coming in for meals. He visited the hospital in the evenings, but Lee didn't go with him.

In one of the nearby fields, two or three women worked every day to remove the heads from red tulips that grew in a long row next to later-blooming pink flowers, with another section which would be white when they opened, so Bert told Lee.

"We'll pick the pink next," he said. "I've promised them for the parade—and the white ones, too, if they open in time. They need a lot of white this year. One of the floats is nearly all white—the Haagen Bulbs Snow Queen."

"Yes, I know. It'll have streaks of yellow, though. I've seen the design."

"Yellow snow?" her uncle said, wrinkling his brow.

"Well, bits of it were yellow on the painting. For shadow, I suppose." She sighed to herself, thinking sadly that now she would not get a chance to be one of the Snow Queen's attendants.

As so often happened, her thoughts drifted back to Lorens and her mind filled with questions. Too many puzzling things had occurred; too many inconsistencies remained for her to put it all aside. Besides, she still ached for him. He haunted her dreams and most nights she woke in the small hours to find herself alone and lonely.

On Saturday morning, Neil dropped by to see how she was coping. He had been to see Sally the previous evening.

"She must be getting better," he said. "She's starting to worry about her bruises—she's got a black eye now, a real shiner. It'll look great if Miss Tulipland appears with a black eye."

"The bruises will surely have faded by next week," Lee said. "I only hope she'll be well enough to take part in the parade."

"She says she'll do it if it kills her," Neil replied.

Busy making cups of coffee, Lee asked, "Did she mention Lorens?"

"No, she didn't."

"I wondered if she expected him to visit her."

"He'd better not," Neil said grimly. "I think she's getting over all that. If he starts it up again . . . Well, speak of the devil! What does *he* want?"

Lee glanced out of the window, her pulse accelerating as the blue Jaguar slid into the yard. Through the lace curtain she saw Lorens climb out, with

Rikki. Both of them were dressed in black corduroys and matching scarlet sweaters, emphasizing the likeness between tall man and small boy. Shaken by the rush of tenderness that swept through her, Lee closed her eyes tightly for a moment, hearing Neil open the door.

"Good morning," Lorens said. "Is Miss Summerfield here?"

"Yes, she is," Neil said shortly. "Who wants her?"

Astounded by the brusquenesss of his tone, Lee exclaimed, "Neil!" and moved where she could see Lorens. "Good morning. Hello, Rikki. Come in."

"I've never actually met Mr. Van Der Haagen," Neil said, his usually pleasant face set in a glower.

"Then let me introduce you," Lee suggested in an attempt at normality when the whole kitchen vibrated with tension. "Lorens, this is Neil Clayton. He's a friend of the family."

"I know who he is, by name, anyway," Lorens said evenly, and held out his hand. "How do you do."

Neil nodded, deliberately stuffing his hands in his pockets, and after a moment Lorens let his own hand drop, his face twisting with derision.

"And this is Rikki," Lee said with false brightness, drawing the boy forward.

Neil nodded again, managing a half-smile for the child. "Hello, Rikki."

The tension between the two men crawled along Lee's nerves. Neil looked ready to do murder, though to her mind Lorens's slight, sardonic smile was the more dangerous.

"I was just making coffee," she said. "Will you have some?"

"No, we didn't come to intrude," Lorens replied, still trading glances with the stocky young farmer.

155

"Rikki wanted to see you, and I wondered how your aunt and cousin were."

"They're doing very nicely," Neil said before Lee could speak. "Is that all you came for?"

Despite Lorens's apparent relaxation, Lee sensed that his temper was not far from exerting itself. She could feel the vibrations in the air.

"No," he said in a deceptively quiet voice. "I also came to ask Miss Summerfield if she'll let me have a key to her cottage." His green glance flicked to Lee's face. "I'll fix that window for you, before you have a real burglar—assuming that Mr. Clayton has no objections."

Mr. Clayton said nothing, only looked more like a thundercloud.

"That would be very kind of you," Lee said, thankful for an excuse to move to her handbag which lay on the rocking chair. She found the key and took it back to Lorens, who contrived to let his fingers brush hers, sending a jolt like electricity up her arm to her heart.

He must have noted her reaction, for a mocking gleam momentarily lit eyes that seemed to read her mind. She turned away, asking Rikki if he would like a drink.

"I've already said we won't stay," Lorens objected. "I can see we came at an inconvenient moment. Shall I bring the key back, or . . . How long are you likely to be here?"

Horribly aware of Neil's hostility, Lee said, "I don't know. We hope that my aunt and Sally will be home in a day or two, but it depends if they're fit to cope."

"Will you be free for next Saturday?"

"I'm—I'm not really sure," she faltered. "Anyway, I didn't think you'd want me to do that any more."

"You promised," he reminded her.

"I know I did, but—"

"Promised what?" Neil wanted to know. "Have you forgotten it's the Tulip Parade next Saturday? Don't tell me you're going to miss it? I thought that was your sole reason for coming home."

Lorens's eyes glinted and he took a deep breath as if to calm his growing temper. "That's what we're talking about—the parade. Lee agreed to take part on the Haagen Bulbs float. Does she need your permission?"

"No." Neil flushed, looking embarrased. "She can do as she likes, I suppose."

"Thank you," Lorens said tightly, turning back to Lee. "I'll see you get the costume before the day, though I've got to go over to Amsterdam again. Rikki's coming with me, to see his grandparents, aren't you, Rikki?"

The child nodded, obviously wary of the strain among the adults around him.

"Oh, you'll enjoy that," Lee said brightly, and was rewarded by a smile from Rikki.

"Well, I'll let you have the key back some time," Lorens said, bending to take his son's hand. "Come on, Rikki, let's go and see about that window."

Rikki's big green eyes looked meltingly at Lee and she stooped to kiss his cheek. "'Bye, darling. See you soon."

"Okay," Rikki replied, and went quietly out to the yard with his father.

Closing the door with a thud, Neil snorted, "You're pretty friendly with them, aren't you? What's wrong with your window?"

"Lorens broke it, if you must know."

"Oh? And what was he doing at your cottage, anyway? You know what he's like, Lee."

Feeling as though the sun had gone out of her day, Lee watched the Jaguar reverse out of the yard and move off up the road. "That's just the trouble, Neil. I *don't* know what he's like. The more I see him, the more I wonder if I've been wrong."

"That's dangerous thinking," Neil warned. "Everybody knows—"

"Knows what?" she demanded, whirling to face him. "Your mother reminded me it's not wise to believe everything you hear, and from my own knowledge of Lorens—"

"There's no smoke without fire," Neil said. "You know he's made a play for Sally. We both saw them at it. He kissed her, right out in the open. It's not a thing any decent man would do."

"You mean *you* wouldn't," Lee corrected. "Have you made a move yet? Have you told her how you feel?"

Neil looked down at his shoes. "I'm getting around to it. Give me time, Lee. I will say something, eventually."

Lee found herself roped in to help with the back-breaking work of heading tulips and putting them into plastic bags so they could be kept in cold storage until they were needed later that week. She was in the field when Neil brought Sally home, but since Uncle Bert broke off from his work and went to the house Lee decided to let him welcome his daughter alone. She was reluctant to face Sally.

Later, however, she dragged her sore muscles to the house to prepare a quick lunch. Sally was ensconced on the couch in the dark front room, surround by magazines and boxes of chocolates.

"How are you feeling, Sally?" Lee asked.

"I'll feel better when I've washed my hair," Sally said, fingering the lank strands on her shoulders. She looked wan, with the remains of a bruise around her left eye. "Dad said I had to rest today, though."

"Yes, he's right. You want to be fit for Saturday.'"

"Oh, I shall be," Sally said.

That evening, when Bert had gone to visit his wife, who was being kept in the hospital another day or two, Neil came to Far Drove and Lee left him to entertain Sally while she occupied herself with some mending in the kitchen. As she struggled to patch a pair of Bert's work trousers, the wall phone rang sharply, making her prick her finger. She leapt up, swearing, and went to answer the call.

From the strange clickings and blips on the line, she gathered it was long distance.

"Lee?" came Lorens's voice. "It's me. How are you?"

"I'm fine," she replied, finding it necessary to lean on the wall. Just talking to him had a devastating effect on her. "Where are you? You're surely not calling from Amsterdam?"

"Why not?"

"Because it's too expensive! I suppoe you want to know how Sally is. Well, she's recovering nicely. She came home today."

"Lee," he said, and even over hundreds of miles she heard the deep warning note in his voice. "Except as a slight acquaintance and a fellow human being, I'm not the least bit interested in that brainless cousin of yours. I wish you would believe that."

"And *I* wish you'd stop lying about it," she replied, beginning to shake. "You're rather more than a slight acquaintance. I saw you myself, down by the river. Or is it your habit to include kissing as an extra when you give a girl a lift?"

"What?" His voice came so loudly that she winced away from the earpiece. "Lee, I can't hear you properly. What did you say?"

She raised her voice, shouting into the phone, "I said . . . Oh, it doesn't matter. Why *did* you call, anyway?"

"What?"

"I said—why did you phone?!"

"Why do you think?" he yelled back.

Holding the phone away from her stinging ear, Lee glared at it before saying into the mouthpiece, "There's no need to shout. I can hear you perfectly well."

"Oh, this is useless," he said in exasperation. "The wonders of bloody modern technology. Did you say you can hear me? Well, just listen. I don't know where you got the idea I was mixed up with Sally. I hardly know the girl. Yes, I took her out to lunch once, but only to ask her some questions about you. Did you get that?"

"Yes!" Lee said loudly.

"Well, do you believe me?"

"I don't know."

"What?"

"I said I don't know!" she screamed. "Oh, go away, Lorens! Leave me alone!" She slammed the phone back onto the hook and leaned against the wall, trembling with reaction.

Then the door opened, and she jumped away from the wall, catching a glimpse of both Neil and Sally before she turned her back on them and picked up the kettle. "Do you want coffee?"

"Who were you shouting at?" Neil asked. "Someone on the phone?"

"It was a bad line," Lee said, wishing they would go away and leave her with her misery.

"It wasn't mother, was it?" Neil said.

"No. No, it was Lorens, actually."

"Oh, was it?" he said grimly. "What did *he* want? I suppose you told him Sally was home. Well, if he shows his face around here, I'll . . ."

Taking a deep breath, Lee recovered her composure and looked around. "He's in Amsterdam, Neil, so stop bristling."

Sally, pale-faced and big-eyed as a child, was watching them with a half-frightened look on her face. "What would you do?" she asked in a hushed voice, her gaze fixed on Neil. "What would you do if he came here?"

Neil flushed, flexing his hands. "I wouldn't be very pleased."

"Why not?"

"Well . . ." He shifted uncomfortably, unable to look at her.

"Oh, for goodness sake!" Lee cried. "If you don't tell her, *I* will."

"You don't have to tell me!" Sally broke in, a tear dripping down her cheek. "I know what it is! Now that you're back, he can't make up his mind between us. Oh, why did you have to come back, Lee? Why?"

Lee stared at her in bewilderment. "Are you talking about Neil? You surely don't think that he and I . . . Sally, that's crazy!"

"Then why was he holding your hand at the Ball?" Sally wept. "Why did he kiss you? I *saw* you, Lee."

Neil had gone scarlet to the ears. He said, "It was only a peck on the cheek. It was nothing, Sally. I don't feel that way about Lee. It's *you* that I . . ."

She was watching him with flooded eyes that reminded Lee of the sun coming through a downpour to create rainbows. "Oh, Neil!" she breathed, and glanced at Lee in sudden consternation. "Oh. Oooooh!" This last was a wail as she flung her hands to her face and darting from the room, thumped up the stairs.

Lee and Neil glanced at each other in astonishment.

"What caused that?" Neil asked.

· "I'm not sure," Lee replied. "Why don't you go and find out?"

He shook his head. "No, not me. Not when she's in that state. You go. I'll wait down here."

Feeling that she would like to shake the man, Lee hurried in pursuit of Sally and found her lying on the bed sobbing loudly, her hands twisted in the folds of the bedspread.

"Sally, don't," Lee begged, sitting beside her. "Don't get so upset. You'll be ill again."

"Where's Neil?" Sally sniffed.

"Waiting downstairs. Waiting for you to put him out of his misery. He's just too desperately shy to tell you how he feels. I wish you'd seen him the other day when Lorens came. I thought he was going to explode."

This news only made Sally howl like a banshee.

"Now stop that!" Lee said sharply. "What's this all about?"

"I thought you wanted him for yourself," Sally muttered into the bed. After a moment, she sat up, then knelt beside Lee with reddened eyes. "Before you went away, I heard mother tell you to stay away from Neil. I thought that was why you left home. At the time, it didn't matter to me, but lately I've seen how super Neil really is. Only he didn't seem to notice me as a woman. I pretended to like Lorens Van Der Haagen in the hopes of forcing Neil to say something. Then *you* came back, and he was so friendly with you, I thought . . ."

Lee groaned inwardly. "Of course he's friendly with me, you idiot! He can be relaxed with me. But *you* matter to him so much he's scared of doing or saying the wrong thing, so he does nothing."

"Oh, blast!" Sally wept, covering her eyes with her hands. "What have I done, Lee? What have I done?"

Feeling very much the older, Lee laid her arm around her cousin's shaking shoulders. "Nothing that can't be undone. Dry your eyes now. Come down and talk to Neil. All he needs is some encouragement. He might have spoken up before now if he hadn't been so convinced you were interested in—"

"I've only been alone with Lorens twice," Sally muttered, wiping her eyes.

Lee couldn't help it; she had to know. "Like the time by the river? The day I came home?"

"Yes," Sally said dully. "I suppose Neil told you about that. Oh, I was mad at him that day. I thought I'd stir him up a bit. I persuaded Lorens to stop, where I knew Neil would see us, and . . . and I cajoled him into kissing me. But I think he guessed I was doing it to shock Neil because afterward he said I was too old to play games like that."

Lee's arm had removed itself from comforting her cousin. She had misunderstood everything Sally had said and, worse, she had thoroughly misjudged Lorens.

"I kept letting Neil think I was going to meet Lorens," Sally was saying, "but actually I never saw him again until the Ball. And then when Neil went to sit with you I was so furious I thought I'd get my own back by asking Lorens to dance."

"Oh, Sally, you little fool!" Lee sighed.

"And that's not all," Sally sniffed. "You haven't heard the worst yet. After I saw you with Neil at Highdyke that Sunday, I was so jealous that I—I phoned the Mill House. Lorens wasn't at home, but his housekeeper must have told him I'd called, because the next day he turned up at the boutique to see what I wanted. He took me to lunch. And I said . . ." Drowned eyes stared unhappily at Lee. "I said a lot of awful things about you. I said you'd always hated us, always tried to spoil things for me, and now you were trying to lure Neil away. And if you couldn't get him then you'd probably settle for a rich man who owned the Mill House, because you'd always fancied living at the Mill House."

Stunned, Lee jumped up from the bed. "Oh, Sally, you didn't! You couldn't!"

"Forgive me," Sally begged. "Oh, please forgive me, Lee. He didn't seem angry. I'm not sure he even believed me."

"Of course he believed you!" At last she understood just why Lorens had been in such a vile temper that night. *It amuses you to have me running around after you, doesn't it*? he had said, and later, *Every trick in the book. Don't you ever give up*? Oh, Lorens. Lorens!

164

"But it doesn't really matter, does it?" Sally said hopefully. "I mean, you've always been so scathing about him."

"Did you tell him that, too?" Lee demanded.

"Yes, I did. It's the truth. You did keep saying he was an—an unprincipled brute. So why have you been seeing him? If not because of Neil, then why?"

"Because I thought it would distract him from you!" Lee said angrily. "Oh, good grief, Sally!" In despair, she sank into a chair, holding her aching head. "Why didn't I trust my instinct? Lorens is marvelous. And between us we've hurt him terribly."

"Well, I'm sorry," Sally said dully. "I didn't know what would happen. All I wanted was for Neil to notice me."

"Then you ought to be very happy. For heaven's sake, go down and talk to him. Let's at least one of us gain something from this mess we've made between us."

"I'll just wash my face," Sally said, and made for the bathroom.

Lee stayed in the chair, despair coloring her thoughts.

Later, when eventually she went down to the kitchen, her uncle had returned with the news that Aunt Jinnie was to be allowed home the next day. But that was not the only cause of the happy atmosphere; Sally and Neil kept sharing secret looks and when Neil took his leave Sally went out to the yard with him and spent half an hour saying goodnight.

Cleaning the house in preparation for Aunt Jinnie's return, Lee sensed that Sally's mood hovered between guilt and elation. At least they managed not to argue, which was a relief, for Lee's nerves felt raw.

She was further relieved when her aunt's home-coming went smoothly. Jinnie had her ribs well strapped, but she had been up and about at the hospital and was not inclined to be treated as a total invalid. However, she seemed grateful that Lee had stepped in to help, and for once she kept her sharp tongue under control.

Several people from the Festival Committee had phoned or visited Sally, anxious about Miss Tulip-land's health. Everyone advised rest before the hectic weekend and, happy in her personal life at last, Sally seemed not to mind too much that her deputy had the limelight in the few days before the parade.

Lee decided to stay and help at the farm until after the weekend, though research for her book took her away a few times. She visited the churches which were holding their own flower festivals, the buildings filled with beautiful fragrant arrangements. The whole town was in festive mood, with bunting being erected and a fairground full of people gathering.

But from Thursday night on activity centered in the big sheds where the floats were being decorated. On Friday evening, Lee went to the sheds and saw the dozens of helpers climbing on scaffolding which had been built around the foats. Big plastic bags bulging with tulip heads of all colors lay around the floor, while helpers fixed each individual head with a big metal pin, slowly covering every inch of the straw.

In the center of the shed, scaffolding surrounded the vast figure of the Snow Queen, whose face was covered with pink tulips except for two slanting dark eyes and a cruel slash of scarlet mouth. The queen's flowing cloak and gown were being done in white tulips, as was the curling front of the sleigh and all the rest of the float. The two big huskies pulling from the separate front section were orangey-brown, with red tongues hanging out.

When Lee arrived, she marveled at the industry involved, and at the cheerful spirit among groups working on the various floats. But she was puzzled by the gaps on the Haagen Bulbs entry: straw still showed where, according to the design, yellow tulips should have been placed as highlights among the white.

"Oh, good," sighed a familiar voice, and Lee found herself looking at Gail's smiling face and disordered red curls. "Another pair of hands. Here, grab a box of pins. There's more white tulips over there. Or are you just going to stand there and watch the rest of us work?"

Laughing, Lee accepted the challenge, dragging a bag of white tulip heads where she could reach them to make more snow beneath the sleigh. "What are you doing here, anyway?"

"Earning a bit of pin money," Gail said. "Literally, pin money. I suppose you're researching."

"That was the general idea," Lee agreed. "It's all work in here, isn't it? The real pull-together spirit. How long will everyone stay?"

"Until the job's done. And *then* the flower arrangers have to do their bit. It's often two or three in the morning before they're finished."

"Rather them than me," said Lee. "But where are the yellow tulips? We can't leave these gaps."

Gail shrugged. "We've been told not to do the yellow yet. Don't ask me why. This is the Haagen Bulbs float, you know. I gather Rikki Van Der Haagen's going to be on it, with six pretty girls."

The reminder brought back Lee's depression. "Yes, so I heard." Pointless to say that she had been asked to provide some of the glamor on this float. Since she had seen no sign of any costume she assumed Lorens had changed his mind. After all, the last thing she had said to him—no, *yelled* at him on the phone—was *Leave me alone.*

For a while they worked on, exchanging good-humored conversation with others pinning tulips around them, some perched on scaffolding because, though the floats were sturdy, only certain places could be stepped on safely. In other places, a careless foot might rip right through the straw matting and ruin months of work.

"Oh my," Gail muttered, looking toward the big doors that stood open. "Look who's coming. The big boss himself, probably checking up on us. Do you want to leave?"

Through the crowd of people, scaffolding, and half-decorated floats, Lee saw Lorens approaching with two or three other men, all of them carrying two more of the bulging sacks. Across the Snow Queen's sleigh a pair of green eyes met Lee's levelly, unsurprised to see her there, and her heart spasmed painfully.

The shorter man beside Lorens said, "Now you can fill those gaps, folks. Pass a couple of these bags to the other side, will you?"

Such was his air of importance, allied with the big grin on his face, that everyone within earshot looked curiously at the plastic bags, and as one reached Gail and Lee a voice not far away said in awe, "They're blue!"

Gail opened the neck of the sack and Lee saw inside thousands of those blue tulip heads, like the ones Lorens had given her weeks before. She glanced back at him and saw one corner of his mouth lift in a mocking, sad little smile.

"Yes, we're privileged," the other man said. "The first appearance of a new strain raised by Haagen Bulbs in Holland. Fix them carefully, folks. They're going to create a sensation tomorrow."

Ten

Lee stared into the sack of blue tulips, deaf to the noise and bustle around her as Gail and the rest began to fix blue shadows among the white snow. Only now did she fully appreciate what a rare gift those tulips had been, brought especially from Holland just for her.

"I phoned the farm and they said I'd find you here," Lorens's voice said quietly from beside her. "I've got your costume in my car. Do you want to come and get it?"

Lee nodded, unable to speak, and ignoring Gail's curious glance she followed Lorens from the shed out to the space where lamps shed light over a gathering of parked cars. He opened the door of the Jaguar and took out a package, offering it to her.

"It would be best if you got someone else," Lee said wearily. "There must be plenty of girls who'd be thrilled to do it."

"Rikki only knows you," Lorens said. "He's a bit scared of being on his own among a crowd of strangers. You might be able to let *me* down, Lee, but don't disappoint Rikki."

Hurt, she looked at him squarely for the first time. "I didn't mean to 'let you down.' I just think—"

"You needn't worry," he broke in. "I won't be there. I've got to attend the civic luncheon and stay with the local dignitaries. I was hoping you'd mind Rikki for me tomorrow. I could bring him to the farm early and then you could take him to the field and get him into his costume and watch over him during the parade . . . I think you owe me that much, Lee."

Pain wrenched through her. Yes, he was right. She owed him something for the way she had behaved, misjudging him, listening to gossip, not to mention toying with his feelings. She was dismally certain that she had hurt him too much for him ever to forgive her.

Avoiding his eyes, she took the package. "All right, I'll do that. Lorens . . . I'm sorry."

"It's a bit late for that," he said, and got into his car.

Lee watched the Jaguar move out of sight, her heart dying a little inside her. She could never explain. He believed she was in love with Neil. Even if she told him the truth, the fact remained that she had set out, quite cold-bloodedly, to fascinate him solely to take his attention from Sally, when actually he had never been interested in Sally. Lee would never forgive herself for cheating him, if only for a brief time.

Unable to face Gail's questions and the happy camaraderie in the shed, she took her costume and went back to the farm.

Parade day dawned bright and cloudless. From early morning the local radio broadcast bulletins of the rising excitement in Spalding. People poured in by car, bus, and train. A vast market had sprung up in the streets overnight; the floats had been assembled on the Halley Stewart field and could be viewed for an entrance fee; and thousands gathered among the delights of Springfields Gardens, where a country fair had been set up. There was plenty to see and do before the parade itself wound through the streets.

Naturally attention at Far Drove centered on Sally that morning. She had a full weekend of events to attend, but she seemed eager for the experience and what bruises remained were soon covered by makeup. Lee helped her fix her hair, letting it fall pale and shining around shoulders left bare by a midnight-blue gown which was part of her prize. Over it went the Miss Tulipland sash, the pale blue cloak, and finally the glittering tiara.

Since Aunt Jinnie was not yet fit to stand up to the rigors of parade day, she had to be content to watch her daughter leave in the official Rolls-Royce—with Neil, who was practically bursting with pride as he accompanied his future wife to her duties.

"It's so good to see her so happy," Aunt Jinnie said as she and Lee waved good luck to the pair. "They make a lovely couple, don't they? Oh, what are you looking so mournful about, Lee? Can't you be happy for Sally?"

"I am, Aunt Jinnie," Lee said. "I'm thrilled for her."

"Well, I wish you'd look a bit more like it," Aunt Jinnie chafed. "The girls on the floats are supposed to look happy. Oh . . . here's Mr. Van Der Haagen. You look after him. I don't want to miss what they're saying on the radio."

Rikki leapt out of the Jaguar and came running excitedly to where Lee stood. He was clutching a package containing his costume.

"I'm glad you're coming with me," he told her, reaching for her hand. "I'm going to be the only boy on our float—the boy the Snow Queen stole."

"Yes, I know," Lee said with a smile.

Lorens had remained in the car, though he had opened his window to lean an elbow out. He looked elegant in a formal suit of dark gray with a white shirt and striped tie, ready for the civic luncheon at which he would be one of the VIPs.

"How are you getting into town?" he asked. "You may have trouble parking."

"Yes, I know," Lee said. "Uncle Bert will drop us off at the field. He and Aunt Jinnie aren't going to the parade. She's not really well enough."

"In that case, tell him not to worry about collecting you. I'll bring you home when it's over. Or is Clayton doing that?"

Tensed against a stupid desire to burst into tears, Lee said, "Neil's got other things to think about today."

"Like what? Oh—he's driving one of the floats, isn't he?"

"Yes, he is. You must have passed the official Rolls along the road. Neil was in it."

"I saw it, but I didn't see who the passengers were. So he's gone with Sally?"

"That's where he belongs," Lee said, her voice catching on the distress in her throat.

For a moment his eyes clouded, then he said, "I'm sorry, Lee."

"For what?" Lee croaked. "I'm glad they finally got things settled between them. It's what everyone's been hoping for—including me."

A small familiar frown puckered between his brows. "You mean that?"

173

"Yes, I do."

Lorens glanced at his son, obviously realizing that Rikki was listening to every word; then his eyes met Lee's again, narrowed with speculation. "We must talk," he said. "Later."

"Yes, all right," Lee agreed, stepping away from the car. She stood for a while with Rikki's small hand in hers as Lorens drove away. She felt too full to speak or move, afraid of bringing her tears nearer the surface. Lorens deserved explanations, of course he did, and she would give them to him, humbly and honestly, without hope of a good ending. When he knew the truth he would probably never want to see her again.

After an early lunch, Bert drove Lee and Rikki into the crowded town where traffic moved at a snail's pace among people walking in the roads around market stalls and vendors' pitches. Rikki exclaimed at the sight of a big ferris wheel in the fairground, with music blasting from steam organs, and at the tiny monkeys clinging to the neck of a man offering photographs. All the people who could make money from a big crowd were there, though many of them would give their proceeds to charity. Hundreds of thousands of people thronged the small town.

Outside the Halley Stewart field, long lines waited to get in to see the floats, but Lee and Rikki were allowed in through a side entrance when they showed the official pass that Rikki had with him. More crowds jostled beyond the gate, outside the central arena where the floats waited in all their colorful glory, every feature of the fairytale characters outlined in varying tulip colors.

174

A loudspeaker made announcements, cameras clicked, and crowds sat in a grandstand waiting for the start of the parade. At the perimeter of the fields, stalls and tents had been joined by vending vans, with people buying ice cream and cold drinks, or wandering into the big tents to look at exhibitions.

A few inquiries led Lee through the crowd, with Rikki hanging on to her hand, to a tent that had been set up in the background to provide changing facilities. Here they were met by a Haagen Bulbs representative, who introduced them to the five girls, employees of the firm, who were to accompany them on the Snow Queen float.

"What a crush!" one of the girls exclaimed. "They say there's over half a million people in town today. Oh, is this Mr. Van Der Haagen's little boy? Hello, Rikki. You sure look like your Daddy." Straightening, she looked curiously at Lee. "You don't work with us, do you?"

"No," said Lee. "I got roped in as an extra."

"She's my Dad's girlfriend," Rikki announced in a piping voice that brought a momentary hush to the group. "Come on, Lee. Let's get changed."

Only too glad to hide her confusion in action, Lee helped him out of his clothes and into blue cotton trousers and a white shirt, worn with clogs on his feet, and a little blue cap. Then she herself wriggled into the white gown of a Snow Queen's attendant. It was very loose and quite thin, draping against her figure while leaving her arms bare, with a deep revealing V at the front. With it went a spiky silver headdress that was a smaller replica of the ice crown worn by the gigantic figure on the float.

175

Eventually they were called onto the sunlit field, where a passage opened in the smiling crowd to let them through the barrier onto open grass where the floats stood. Bands in colorful uniforms marched in to their own music, silver balloons floated occasionally skyward, and people in period costume rode a collection of old-fashioned bicycles.

Lee became aware of a special buzz of excitement near the Haagen Bulbs float as photographers, both on the field and among the crowd, jostled to get pictures that included the blue tulips. Now the two halves of the float had been joined together to form a sixty-foot-long spectacle. A tractor hidden between the two huskies and beneath the "snow" was attached to the trailer on which the sleigh had been built. At the rear of the float, the massive and evil Snow Queen, her cloak flowing, grinned madly as she whipped up the dogs.

When all the bands had taken their place in the center of the field, fresh shouts and applause accompanied the arrival of Miss Tulipland and her deputy. Sally was escorted into the middle of the field, helped into a decorated forklift truck, and raised high above the arena. Through the loudspeakers her voice lifted confidently in a few words welcoming the visitors; then she was helped from the forklift high onto her Fairy Queen float. She sat on the central turret of a fairy castle emerging from a forest of huge flowers. Big red and white toadstools on the front of the float bore seats for children dressed as elves and fairies.

The Haagen Bulbs driver arrived and clambered into the tractor between the two huskies, only his head visible after he was seated. Then a man came and helped Rikki up to his central seat in front of the Snow Queen, with Lee not far away and another dark-haired girl on the far side. The remaining four girls took their places along the float, while around the field other riders climbed aboard the huge tulip-covered structures.

"Okay?" Lee asked Rikki, who nodded excitedly, his face bright as he began to wave to the crowds crushing against the barriers.

As Lee had feared, her seat wasn't very comfortable, just a flat square with a semicircular metal backrest. But Geoff Dodds the blacksmith had also provided a strategic handle for each rider to hang on to. Lee soon forgot her discomfort as the first float set off at a walking pace, edging slowly out of the field with the invisible Neil driving his Fairy Queen to the acclamation of the crowds.

The MC described each float, naming both sponsor and riders, and in between the bands marched, playing lively tunes. There was the grinning Puss In Boots, a giant with a beanstalk, Cinderella in a pumpkin coach, the Babes in the Wood with a gingerbread house and a witch. Altogether, twenty of the massive floats, ablaze with color and adorned with waving riders, eased out of the field and into the streets of Spalding. On either side, crowds cheered and waved, bands played, balloons were flying, tulips being hurled, and everywhere cameras and more cameras clicked as people recorded moments from the big day.

It was a long, slow, exhilarating ride. Laughing, Lee waved back to the happy crowds, glancing every so often at Rikki, who was equally enjoying himself. If only it could go on, she thought, but thrust the wish away. Lately she had kept returning to that phrase of despair "if only," and it didn't do the least good. What had happened between her and Lorens had happened, and no amount of wishful thinking could alter it.

On the narrow bridge that crossed the deep river, the float came to a halt as some slight hitch occurred up ahead. There on the water floated two huge tulip swans to add to the figures which decorated the town itself. Crowds lined the route ahead and behind, calling to the riders on the temporarily halted floats which by then spread for nearly a mile, from the police horses leading the Miss Tulipland float to the last band bringing up the rear. But there on the bridge lay a small island of relative peace.

"Rikki," Lee said quietly, laying a hand on the child's arm to make him look at her. "You mustn't say I'm your Dad's girlfriend."

"Why not?" Rikki demanded. "It's what he told me to say."

"When was this?" Lee asked.

"This morning, before we left home. Oh! We're moving again!"

With a slight shudder that made Lee cling to her supportive handle, the float edged forward once more, across the bridge and down the riverside road, with people cheering all the way.

Slowly, the parade made its vivid and noisy way to the outskirts of town and the big arena at Springfields Gardens, where another huge crowd waited to see the bands and the floats do a complete circuit of the grounds before turning back toward town. Lee saw the dignitaries on the VIP stand, but though she searched for Lorens's tall figure as she smiled and waved, she did not see him.

"Do you see Dad?" Rikki asked. "He said he'd be here."

"No, I don't," said Lee, troubled. Where could Lorens be? The float moved so slowly that if he had been on the stand she would have picked him out with ease.

They returned to town by a different route, where people had waited for hours to see the passing show. With the sun shining and everyone full of high spirits, the ride was a joy. Drivers craned to see as they edged their monster trailers through narrow, crowd-lined streets, and comic antics among the bandsmen brought gales of laughter. People stood at windows, on rooftops, some even perched in the trees, using every available vantage point.

As they approached the Halley Stewart field and the end of the ride, Lee realized that her arms ached from waving and another part of her anatomy was almost numb from being attached to that hard seat for four hours. On the field, most of the crowd had regathered to see the floats come safely home. The Snow Queen, with her captive boy and her six attendants, finally came to a halt at the place in the circle where they had begun.

"Just wait a minute," Lee instructed Rikki. "Let me get down first and then I'll give you a hand."

But as she began to ease out of her seat she hesitated, for Lorens stood beside the float, his arms out to help her. He wore a challenging expression that turned her heart over.

She gave him one of her hands, searching for a safe foothold on the hidden struts. But she was so stiff she had to virtually launch herself and leap to the ground, only prevented from falling by the strength of Lorens's arms around her. He held her tight for a moment, her lightly clad body pressed to that elegant suit.

"All right?" he murmured.

"Yes, I'm fine," she muttered, embarrassed to be so close to him in front of hundreds of witnesses as the crowd swirled and chattered. He released her and as she stretched her aching legs he helped Rikki down, too. The other girls were being assisted by other willing hands.

"Well, did you enjoy it?" Lorens asked.

"Oh, yes!" Rikki cried, and went on to describe funny things he had seen, making Lorens laugh.

Watching him, so tall and fine and handsome with his fair hair bathed in sunlight, Lee felt unnerved by that moment in his arms. It made her ache for more, an ache that was worse to bear than any pain from cramped muscles.

"We'd better go and get changed," she said.

"No, not yet," Lorens objected. "We're all having tea in one of the tents. You must be ready for a drink."

"I'm dying of thirst!" Rikki declared.

So Lee had no choice but to go with them into the cool shade of the tent where hot drinks and refreshments had been organized for all the participants and their families. She heard Lorens thank the other five girls for their help. He said they had all looked wonderful, and every one of them laughed and blushed at being noticed by their attractive managing director.

A cup of tea had never tasted better, Lee decided as she let the hot liquid trickle down her throat. She wasn't hungry, but Rikki dived into rolls and cakes as if he hadn't eaten for days, while his father looked on smiling. Lorens was in a very light mood, presumably because of the success of the day. His blue tulips had caused the expected stir and the Van Der Haagen name had been given a good airing.

Across the tent, Lee saw Sally enjoying the full attention of officials, with Neil never far from her side, watching her as if she were a banquet and he a starving man. The sight brought a lump to Lee's throat; once Lorens had looked at *her* like that. Why had she been too blind to believe it?

"Lee," he said softly, drawing her attention back to his face, where that same look of undisguised longing played havoc with her insides. "If you'd like to get Rikki out of that get-up now, I'll meet you behind the organizer's caravan. My car's there."

Distracted by the message in his eyes, it took her a moment to hear what he had said. "Oh—yes, all right. Have you finished, Rikki!"

"Phew!" Rikki exclaimed, patting his stomach. "Yes, I'm full."

Traffic jammed the town as people tried to get away after the celebrations. At every junction, uniformed police directed cars and buses, while pedestrians dodged in and out adding an extra hazard. Lorens kept his patience, sitting relaxed at the wheel with Lee beside him and Rikki on the back seat yawning.

Eventually they were off the main roads and onto the quieter lane which followed the river on its way to Far Drove.

"You're tired, I suppose," Lorens said.

"Yes, I am," Lee admitted. "I'm longing for a soak in a hot bath."

"And then?" He smiled slightly at her look of incomprehension. "I'm trying to ask you to spend the evening with me. Are you surprised? You did say we could talk, and it will be easier without a certain small person." An over-the-shoulder gesture indicated his son. "I'll drop you off, go home and get Rikki settled, and then come back for you later. Okay?"

"Okay," Lee agreed, her heart heavy. As chance would have it, they were just passing the side track where she had stopped that day so many eons ago and seen Lorens with Sally. If only she hadn't jumped to conclusions . . . But there she went again, wishful thinking.

He did not turn into the yard but left her at the entrance, promising to be back in a couple of hours at the latest. Aware that he was watching, Lee walked across the yard, feeling obliged to glance back before she reached the house.

Rikki waved from the car and Lorens, gravely and deliberately, blew her a kiss. Feeling embarrassed, Lee went in to face questions from her aunt and uncle about her day. They had followed it all on the radio and wanted to know how Sally had coped.

"She was doing fine when I last saw her," Lee said. "She made a lovely tulip queen."

"I knew she would," Aunt Jinnie said smugly. "Oh, I wish I could have been there. To see both of you. *Both* my girls in the tulip parade. And I see Mr. Van Der Haagen brought you home. I thought he would. Something going on there, isn't it? I *told* you he was a nice man."

Lee remembered. She also remembered that she hadn't believed her aunt.

"I'm seeing him later," she said. "Do you mind if I have a bath?"

"Lee, love," her uncle said firmly. "This is your *home.* "

Somehow, among accidents and flower parades and Sally finally getting together with Neil, Lee's relationship with the Freemans seemed to have changed. Whatever the cause, she had been oddly touched to hear her aunt talk about "my girls." It was the first time she could remeber being included in such a context.

Soaking her muscles in a hot bath, she thought about the coming evening. How could she tell Lorens the truth without making Sally look like a fool? It was true that Sally's feather-brained schemes and imaginings had caused a lot of the trouble, but nothing could excuse Lee's own machinations. She had a feeling that her date with Lorens would turn out to be one of the shortest on record. When he found out she had planned to deceive him, he would bring her straight home and that would be that.

She took time over her grooming, mostly to boost her morale. Since the only slightly dressy outfit she had brought from the cottage was a pale green skirt and top in a soft, silky material, she had no choice about what to wear. Her dark hair was clean and shining, swinging around her face when she shook her head. With high-heeled sandals and a white linen jacket, she looked like a cool career woman. That was how she wanted it. There must be no breaking down tonight, or Lorens might think that she was using tears again as a trick to soften him.

Going downstairs, she found her family and Neil all gathered round the kitchen table while Sally recounted her day's experiences. Clearly she had enjoyed herself and well survived the strenuous day.

"You look super, Lee," she said, free to be generous now that she no longer saw Lee as a rival. "Did you enjoy the parade, too? Oh, and I forgot to tell you, Mum, at the luncheon, the mayor . . ."

The story was still being told when Lorens's car appeared in the yard and Lee excused herself amid cries of, "Have a good time," and from Sally a significant,"Good luck."

Lorens had changed his formal suit for dark slacks and an oatmeal jacket, worn with a pale yellow shirt. The faint scent of his aftershave brought back heady memories as Lee slid into the car beside him.

Without a word, he back out of the yard and drove off, carrying her to face her dreaded fate. For a while they traveled in silence, past fields full of headless tulips.

"You don't seem exactly overjoyed with my company," he remarked eventually. "Nothing to say?"

"Too much," Lee said in a low voice. "I don't know where to start."

"Then may I suggest you begin by assuring me you have not, and never did have, any deep and meaningful relationship with Neil Clayton?"

She caught her breath, chancing a glance at his face and finding it bland, telling her nothing. "Of course I didn't!"

"Well, that's good. I admit I *was* beginning to wonder about that myself. Even before he and Sally told me the whole story at lunchtime."

"Oh." It came out on a sigh heavy with relief. "Then you know that Sally misunderstood—"

"She wasn't the only one though, was she? I gather I got branded a filthy lecher before you even knew me. On what evidence, Lee? Local gossip and the fact that you saw me kiss Sally? I'll remind you that I'm a single man, and therefore free to do as I

184

please. If I had a permanent relationship with someone it would be different, but I don't have that sort of relationship, not at the moment."

"I'm aware of that," Lee said dully, unable to resist adding, "And you told me you never would have. You said one fiasco was enough."

He slanted her an unreadable look. "Did I? When?"

In her own mind the memory of that night was all too clear—his fury, his kisses, his hands and mouth on her flesh. A shiver ran through her. "It doesn't matter when."

"I agree that's one night I'd prefer to forget, too," Lorens said quietly. "My only excuse is that I was very angry at the time. And not only angry—I'd spent the entire evening thinking you were with Clayton. I hope you'll forgive me."

"Oh, Lorens—" She couldn't go on for the tears that choked her. "Stop the car."

"What?"

"I said stop the car. Please!"

He drew up beside woods that lay on either side of a winding country lane, isolated and peaceful in the evening air.

"Well?" he asked, turning to lean his elbow on the back of his seat. "Why did you want me to stop?"

"So you won't have so far to go back," Lee muttered, twisting her hands in her lap. The tears in her head swelled behind her eyes, stinging hotly. "Oh, hell! I promised myself I wouldn't cry. Excuse me."

She hurriedly left the car, taking deep breaths to calm herself as she walked in among the trees. The sun had gone, leaving the sky pale and calm, and a lone bird twittered crossly at having his territory disturbed by humans. Leaning on a tree, Lee forced back the tears, shaking out her hair as Lorens came across the grass behind her.

His hands rubbed her shoulders in a comforting way as he rested his cheek on her hair, saying softly, "What's the trouble, love? Tell me."

"There's something you ought to know," she croaked, and drew another deep, shuddering breath. "I set out, quite calmly, to distract you from Sally. I suppose—I suppose you could say I was trying to seduce you, playing at what I thought was your own game."

"Because of the Mill House?" he asked.

Pulling away, she whirled to face him, crying, "No, *not* because of the Mill House! It's true I've always thought it was a lovely house, but if you seriously think I could petend to care about someone just for a piece of property then you're wrong. If you lived in a one-room hovel, I'd—" She stopped herself, appalled by what she had nearly blurted out.

"You'd what?" he prompted.

Drawing herself up, Lee took a fresh hold of her runaway emotions. "Did you understand what I said? I deliberately set out to—"

"To make me fall in love with you," he finished for her, his voice grave though a suspicion of laughter sparked in his eyes. "You succeeded."

"I was afraid of that," she said wretchedly. "You're not listening to me. Lorens. I didn't like you one bit. At least . . . I didn't like what I knew of your reputation. I kept watching your technique, thinking how clever you were. I honestly believed you were just angling to add me to your list of conquests. I never stopped to consider you might be human enough to be hurt. I was so busy being clever I outsmarted myself. It was only when you were so worried about me, that day after the Ball, that I began to realize . . ." The words trailed off as the expression in his eyes reached through her recital and made pain wrench through her. "Don't look at me like that. Don't—"

And then there were no more words. There was only Lorens, kissing her in the way only Lorens could, with his arms warmly around her holding her possessively close to the firmness of his body. A little groan escaped Lee as she wrapped her arms around him and clung to him with all her strength, returning his kisses with passionate despair.

After a while, he lifted his head and gazed down at her with burning eyes. "Now tell me you don't love me. Say that, Lee, and I'll let you go. Only tell the truth, once and for all."

She could hardly see him for a glaze of scalding tears. "Of course I love you. I love you so much I hurt. I've loved you for a long time, if only I'd let myself believe it. But Lorens—"

His mouth stopped the protests, bringing waves of emotion from deep inside her until she trembled and pressed closer to him. Eventually she buried her face in the curve of his throat, weeping against him.

"That's all that matters," he said, his lips moving near her ear. "How we feel *now*. How it began isn't important. Nor how stupid we've both been in the meantime." He hugged her more closely, giving a shaky laugh. "Do you know, there've been times when I've even been jealous of Rikki? You kept touching him and kissing him, when I'd have given my right arm for a little of your affection. Come on, let's go."

"Go where?" she asked, lifting her head.

"You'll see," he said, and kissed her again before leading her back to the car where he presented her with a clean handkerchief.

Spalding was quieter now, resting after the day's exertions in preparation for another day of festivity tomorrow. Bunting fluttered and at street junctions tulip-covered figures still drew attention from passersby as people gathered for parties and private celebrations.

Eventually the car moved onto the long road away from town, heading, Lee assumed, for the Mill House.

"I thought you'd be angry," she said, clutching his damp handkerchief in her hands. "Honestly, Lorens, I thought some terrible things about you."

"So did I about you," he replied. "Would it make you feel better if we argued about which of us was most at fault?"

"No, not really."

"Besides, I knew all along that something wasn't quite right. It only made me more intrigued. I fell for you the first time we met, you know. I thought you felt the same."

"I did," she admitted brokenly. "But I didn't believe you really cared. I didn't start to believe that until after that awful night when everything went wrong. I wanted to come and see you, but I was too afraid. If Rikki hadn't turned up at the cottage when he did—"

"Thank God for Rikki," Lorens said with a smile, "though I must say he makes an unlikely Cupid. Incidentally, I think you ought to know that my son has his eye on you as a stepmother. He needs someone. With Elena in Switzerland he won't see much of her. And a boy needs a mother."

Lee's mind had gone blank. She stared at the darkening fields rushing by. "Yes, but—"

"But of course there's your career. You're going back to New York."

"I don't have to," she said, turning impulsively to him before she realized just what she had said. "I mean . . . to make a really good job of my book I ought to stay and watch the whole process. They're already planning next year's parade. And I haven't done half the research I need to do."

Lorens gave her a slow smile, teasing and tender, but said nothing.

To Lee's surprise, as night crept across the sky, leaving a pale streak in the west, he turned down the lane that led to the cottage. He stopped the car outside the yard and turned to her.

"Have you eaten?"

Breathless, her heart thudding loud in her ears, Lee shook her head.

"Neither have I," Lorens said. "That's why I had Mrs. Rufford make up a hamper. Cold chicken, pâté, some wine . . . I want to be alone with you this evening. How do you feel about that?"

"It sounds wonderful," Lee said, leaning across to kiss him.

They went into the cottage, Lorens bringing the hamper. He still had the key he had borrowed to mend her window and as she went down the hall Lee smelled a fragrance that drew her into the living room. Switching on the light as she entered, she gasped as she saw the flowers that decked the room—all kinds of bright and beautiful blooms arranged with ferns and greenery. Someone had also lit the fire, giving the place a welcoming glow.

"How on earth—" she gasped.

"Magic," Lorens said, putting down the hamper as he drew her farther into the flower-filled room and pointed out the blue tulips which graced one of the vases.

"I didn't realize how special they were," Lee sighed, clasping his hand tightly as she leaned on his shoulder. "Oh, Lorens . . . thank you. It's a lovely surprise."

"When I went to Amsterdam that first time," he told her, "my father gave me the honor of naming this new strain. They've been twenty years in the process of coming to perfection, and then we couldn't be sure they wouldn't revert to type until they'd bloomed true for seven years. This is the seventh year. They'll be on the market this season. Do you know that I called them?"

"No, what?"

"Lee Summerfield."

As she caught her breath, lifting her head to look at him, Lorens smiled at her in a way that made her feel like melting.

"Only I think I'll change it," he said, taking her in his arms. "I think we'll make it Lee Van Der Haagen now."